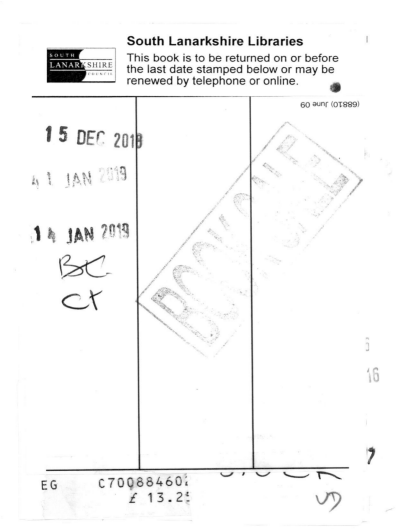

Siege at Hope Wells

When the plague came to Hope Wells, it took the weak and healthy, young and old, good and bad. Within a week the town had become a living hell, but for differing reasons some men still wanted to go there.

Marshal Lincoln Hawk and Nick Mitchell went in search of the outlaw Marvin Sewell. Correspondent Kyle Portman sought a story for his newspaper and Peter Campbell wanted to rescue his wife. The least welcome visitor was Ward Dixon, who saw an opportunity to profit from the developing tragedy. In a desperate time that brought out the best and the worst in humanity, these men become embroiled in a conflict where even the might of the gun won't guarantee survival.

Siege at Hope Wells

Scott Connor

A Black Horse Western

ROBERT HALE · LONDON

Robert Hale Limited
Clerkenwell House
Clerkenwell Green
London EC1R 0HT

www.halebooks.com

The right of Scott Connor to be identified as
author of this work has been asserted by him
in accordance with the Copyright, Designs and
Patents Act 1988

Typeset by
Derek Doyle & Associates, Shaw Heath
Printed and bound in Great Britain by
CPI Antony Rowe, Chippenham and Eastbourne

CHAPTER 1

Hope Wells looked deserted.

Marshal Lincoln Hawk drew his horse to a halt outside the saloon and looked up and down the main drag. Nobody was outside and through the saloon's grimy windows he could see nobody inside either.

It was around noon and a town that boasted a population of 200 and growing, as promised by the town sign, should be showing more life than this. Aside from the saloon Lincoln had already noted a law office, two stables, a mercantile and a hotel, and off the main drag a block structure promised more buildings.

And yet all was quiet.

Lincoln dismounted and headed into the saloon. Tables had been pushed back to one wall to provide an open space in which curled blankets lay, as if people had slept on the saloon floor. With these signs of life cheering him Lincoln went to the bar and banged a fist on the top. He hollered for service.

Silence greeted him.

Shaking his head Lincoln headed back to the saloon doors and while leaning on them he looked for movement and listened intently. But other than the sign outside the hotel opposite creaking back and forth and the buzz from a persistent fly enjoying the growing heat of the day, he saw and heard nothing.

'Where are you?' Lincoln murmured to himself. 'Where are all of you?'

He had been pursuing the outlaw Marvin Sewell for a week through several towns, all the time gaining on him. He reckoned Marvin had holed up here but he was now wondering if he'd veered off to Rocky Bar. But then, as if in answer to his question, the distant clop of hoofs sounded.

As the rider was getting closer Lincoln risked edging out through the doorway. The rider matched Marvin's description, so he slipped back into the saloon, then moved to the window where, with his back to the wall, he kept in the shadows and watched Marvin ride along. Like Lincoln, he was looking around, staring through windows and into open doorways as he searched for signs of life.

His gaze alighted on Lincoln's horse. With a skyward look, presumably in relief, he headed towards the saloon.

As this was the closest Lincoln had got to Marvin, he reckoned that his quarry wouldn't recognize the horse. Even so he took no chances and he sought out the best cover he could find behind the bar.

He heard Marvin dismount, then walk across the boardwalk and come in.

'Who's here?' Marvin called.

The only reply came from the squeaking saloon doors. Footfalls closed on the bar. A clatter sounded as Marvin dropped a saddle-bag. Then he located a discarded whiskey glass and slammed it down while demanding to know who was here.

Lincoln sidled along behind the bar to position himself below his quarry. Then he waited until the banging stopped and the shadow Marvin was casting on the wall turned.

He stood up, his Peacemaker thrust out. Marvin had leaned back against the bar to survey the saloon room, so before he could react Lincoln had thrust cold steel against the back of his neck.

'Marvin Sewell,' Lincoln said, 'you're under arrest.'

'Now why have you gone and done that?' Marvin said with surprising calmness.

'You ran off with five hundred dollars from the White Ridge depot.' The marshal glanced at the bulging saddle-bag on the floor. 'They'd like it back.'

Marvin shrugged. 'And you reckon you can keep me prisoner for the week it'll take to get me back there?'

'It won't be hard.' Lincoln reached over the bar and removed Marvin's gun from its holster. 'I know what you're capable of, and that's not much.'

Marvin sneered as with a firm shove Lincoln pushed him away, then signified that he should leave.

7

He came out from behind the bar and, walking behind him with the saddle-bag draped over a shoulder, he headed to the door.

Marvin walked in a relaxed manner that suggested he was planning something. Sure enough, when he pushed through the doors he grabbed a batwing. Then, while he ducked and leapt to the right, he jerked it backwards aiming to hit Lincoln.

Lincoln neatly side-stepped past the swinging door and followed Marvin, but then he found that Marvin had turned back and was advancing on him. Lincoln jerked backwards, letting Marvin's whirling fist part air before his face. Then he hammered a blow of his own into Marvin's side.

Marvin grunted in pain and dropped to his knees on the boardwalk. That didn't stop Lincoln following through by slipping the saddle-bag from his shoulder and smacking Marvin's face with it, knocking him on his side.

Then he was on him. He dropped the saddle-bag and slapped a heavy hand on Marvin's vest front. He hoisted him up off the boardwalk.

'Get your hands off me,' Marvin muttered, but Lincoln ignored him and slammed him back against the saloon wall where he held him, staring into his eyes.

'That was the only time you jump me. Try it again and you'll learn what pain is. Understood?'

Marvin glared at him with defiance, but when Lincoln tightened his grip he gave a brief nod.

'Yeah, lawman,' he muttered.

Lincoln reckoned Marvin was still showing too much surliness, so when he released his grip he crunched a low blow into Marvin's guts, which made him fold over and stagger forward for a pace. Lincoln stepped behind him, then slapped the sole of his boot to his rump and pushed him on to the hardpan.

Marvin ran forward doubled over, his arms wheeling as he fought to stay on his feet, but he failed and went tumbling, rolling over twice before coming to a halt in a wheel rut. Lincoln followed; then, while standing over him he gave him a moment to gather his breath. But when Marvin got his wits about him he looked across the road.

Lincoln followed his gaze. Three men had arrived. They were standing in front of the hotel across the road, each man standing ten feet from the other but they were all silently watching him.

'I'm US Marshal Lincoln Hawk,' Lincoln called. 'Marvin Sewell is my prisoner and I'll get him out of your way.'

'You won't,' the man on the left of the group said. 'He stays here, as will you.'

'And who are you to stand in my way?'

'I'm Will Garland, mayor of Hope Wells, and nobody, not even a lawman leaves.' He gave an apologetic frown. 'You'll stay here and die with the rest of us.'

'Rocky Bar!' the driver called down, making two of the occupants of the stage peer out of the windows.

9

Nick Mitchell didn't join them, finding nothing exciting about ending the penultimate leg of a journey he'd been reluctant to make. The others were slightly more animated.

Kyle Portman, the fresh-faced young lad sitting beside him, shuffled eagerly on his seat. He claimed he was a special correspondent for the *North Town Times*, and he was heading to Rocky Bar for an important interview. Nick reckoned he wasn't old enough to be allowed to go this far on his own, but he'd kept that thought to himself.

The stiff-backed and black-clad man sitting opposite leaned back in his seat. He hadn't revealed why he was heading west. Any questions Nick had asked and, more interesting, that the correspondent had asked, had been met with an obvious change of subject. He had only reluctantly revealed that he was called Ward Dixon.

Nick didn't mind; silence was preferable to the chatter that had filled the hours on other stage journeys he'd undertaken.

Presently isolated buildings appeared on either side of the stage, followed by the town. With much hollering the stage drew to a halt outside a hotel. Nick bade goodbye to Kyle as he left, then gestured for Ward to disembark next. He declined, so Nick jumped down after Kyle, aiming to enjoy a break.

'You'll all have to get out,' the driver said, looking into the stage. 'This is the end of the journey.'

'I paid to be taken to Hope Wells,' Nick said while from inside the stage this news made Ward become talkative at last.

He bustled out of the stage, gesticulating wildly and making the same complaint as Nick, but with added threats. Nick stood back to see how the debate developed but, other than making Ward get more irate with every rebuff, nothing changed.

It hadn't been the driver's decision.

A line of men stood on the boardwalk with their arms folded and with surly expressions on their faces, which suggested they were looking forward to Ward turning his attention on them.

Accordingly the moment Ward took the driver's advice and moved away to find someone else to complain to, these men stepped forward and surrounded him.

'Like he said,' the nearest man said, 'your journey ends here.'

'But I have to go to Hope Wells,' Ward said.

'Nobody goes to Hope Wells no more. That town is closed.'

'Closed! Why?'

'It's a plague town. Only the dead and the dying are there now.' The man snorted a harsh laugh. 'But when they've all died, you can help us burn the stinking heap to the ground.'

CHAPTER 2

'The plague!' Marshal Lincoln Hawk spluttered. 'What kind of plague?'

The three men looked at each other until one man stepped forward.

'Cholera,' he said.

Lincoln winced. 'That's bad, but I've only been here for a few minutes. I'll—'

'You're not going anywhere. This town is quarantined.'

'You should have thought of that before you let me in.'

Mayor Garland stepped closer and spread his hands.

'I'm sorry. Rocky Bar men are supposed to be patrolling and making sure nobody gets within ten miles of us. But even if they didn't stop you, they'll make sure you don't leave and spread the death.'

'They can try,' Lincoln said, dragging Marvin to his feet. 'But nobody stands in my way.'

'Except for us,' Garland said.

Lincoln considered the three men, none of whom was armed, but they had all drifted close enough for him to see their haggard expressions and their hunched postures.

'You may outnumber me, but you're in no state to stop me.'

'We won't stop you with strength, but we will with words. Don't go. A lawman shouldn't spread our plague.'

Lincoln knew nothing of cholera other than a few terrible old tales he'd heard of a virulent disease that took hold quickly and killed everyone who caught it. But he knew his duty and he couldn't endanger life in the course of bringing a man to justice.

He gave a brief nod. 'I'll need somewhere to lock this one up.'

'Sheriff Bester died yesterday, but he died at home, so the jailhouse will be safe.'

Marvin darted worried looks at everyone, then tried to wrestle himself free of Lincoln's grip. But Lincoln held him tightly, then pushed him on towards the indicated law office.

'Think of it this way,' Lincoln said, gathering up the saddle-bag of stolen money, 'you could be safer in a cell than out here.'

'What if you all die?' Marvin grumbled. 'I'll end up rotting in there.'

'Don't worry. If that looks likely, I'll put a bullet in you and give you a quick end.'

Marvin snorted a harsh laugh, then remained silent as Lincoln moved him on. Despite the assurances Lincoln took deep breaths before he entered the office, as if that might keep the disease away.

As promised, the office was deserted. Lincoln wasted no time in locating the keys, then locking Marvin in a cell and putting the stolen money in a desk. When he left the office two of the men were walking away, giving each other a wide berth.

The third man was approaching. He had been quiet before and unlike the others he didn't balk at being close to Lincoln.

'I'm Doctor Weaver,' he said, his voice strained and hoarse. 'I'm the only man who can save this town.'

Lincoln smiled. 'There's two now.'

Weaver lowered his head and uttered a long sigh.

'It's good to hear you say that. The others have given up hope, but they're wrong to do that. The town can survive this.'

Lincoln noted the doctor's careful choice of words.

'Are you saying the town may survive, but not everyone who lives here?'

'Sadly not, but I hope I acted quickly enough to save us from the worst.' Weaver moved off down the main drag and Lincoln filed in beside him. The doctor gestured to the left and right. 'You won't see many people about. That's the important part of my plan. I'm keeping everyone isolated in the places where they'd usually be.'

'But you're moving around, and me now.'

'Somebody has to, but the disease isn't spread by

people.' Weaver shrugged. 'Although you can catch it from other people.'

'You're not making sense, Doc.'

Weaver stopped and raised his hat to run his fingers through his matted hair while sighing wearily.

'I haven't had much sleep recently and I'm finding it hard to make sense. Perhaps it'd be easier if I showed you.'

Lincoln relented from his questioning and let Weaver lead him on. They walked through the town, seeing nobody, then carried on beyond the edge of town.

After 200 yards Weaver halted and pointed to a fenced-off area. A large wooden building stood there with the double doors facing out on to an expanse of mud, the centre of which had become a dirty pool.

'The wells?' Lincoln asked.

'Sure. They gave the town life but then they brought death. Somehow the water got contaminated and everyone who drank it is in danger. Those who drank the most died the quickest.'

'How could it get contaminated?'

'People live close together here. Human waste's not far away. It just needed a sick newcomer to arrive and the water did the rest.'

While Lincoln looked at the muddy area, imagining the train of events, two men emerged from the building to peer around. Their gazes alighted on the marshal and the doctor. They paced out towards them, skirting the worst of the mud with rifles held low.

15

'So,' Lincoln said to Weaver, 'the way to stop the plague is to stop drinking water?'

Lincoln had meant his question to be a facetious one, to reduce the tension, but Weaver nodded.

'It's a tough solution, but it's the only one that'll work.' Weaver pointed out of town. 'The good folk of Rocky Bar have been ferrying water in to us most days, and in time that'll save us.'

Lincoln was about to reply but the two men had come closer.

'And that means,' one man shouted, brandishing his rifle, 'the end for us.'

Weaver winced. When he spoke his voice was strained, as if he was returning to an old argument.

'It doesn't have to lead to that. You three will still be welcome here.' He looked past the two men to the building. 'Is Brad sick?'

'He don't want no help from a man who's blaming us for everything.'

'Nobody is blaming anybody. The time for that is after we've cleaned up—'

'So you're still claiming the Ellison brothers are unclean.'

The second man barged past the first and wasted no time in swinging his rifle up to aim it at Weaver.

'Take your threats back, Weaver,' he muttered, 'or I'll blast you in two.'

'Where are you going?' Ward Dixon demanded.

'I'm getting a drink while this mess gets sorted out,' Nick Mitchell said. He moved away from Ward

16

and the truculent group of men he was confronting.

'This mess will never get sorted out.' Ward hurried on to join him. 'The stage is going no further. We're stuck here.'

Nick considered him, torn between getting involved in the argument and leaving Ward to deal with it.

'Then I suggest you talk them round.' Nick pointed down the road to a saloon that stood beside a stable. 'When you've done that, I'd be obliged if you'd tell me.'

Nick tipped his hat, then headed off. Behind him Ward muttered to himself before he waded back into the fray with more complaints.

When Nick had crossed the road he glanced over his shoulder and smiled on seeing that Ward was now remonstrating with the driver. Two men were holding him back and another man was drawing the driver away.

With more people being dragged into the argument, Nick reckoned it was sure to go badly for the newcomer as the townsfolk were clearly determined not to let anyone move on to Hope Wells.

When Nick reached the saloon he carried on past the building and headed into the stables.

'Horses are mighty popular today,' the ostler said when Nick had made his request.

Nick narrowed his eyes, reckoning this was the start of an attempt to demand an outrageous price.

'Who else bought one today?'

A steady finger pointed into the depths of the

stable where Kyle, the young man who had accompanied him on the stage, was dealing with his rigging.

'Find me a decent one at a good price,' Nick said, then headed on in the direction indicated.

Kyle had noticed his arrival, but he continued with his task until Nick was standing beside him.

'You had the same idea as I had, then?' Kyle said, his voice low.

'I have, but then again I've always said I was on my way to Hope Wells. You said you had an interview to make here.'

Kyle checked that the ostler was busying himself at the other end of the stable, then leaned towards Nick and winked.

'I do, but I'm a correspondent for the *North Town Times*. I have to be where the biggest story is. And that's at Hope Wells right now.'

'The only thing you'll find at Hope Wells is death.'

'I'm prepared to take that risk to get a first-hand account of the battle for survival in the living hell of a plague town.' Kyle's eyes took on a feverish gleam as presumably he concocted more of his story before he'd even seen the situation, making Nick hope that the gleam would remain due to enthusiasm and not real fever. 'But why are you prepared to take that risk?'

Nick shrugged. 'I just have to get there.'

Kyle considered this, then he gave a smile. 'Then maybe we should go to Hope Wells together.'

Nick sighed. 'I don't suppose I can talk sense into you?'

18

'Nope.'

'Then I guess the two of us are riding together.'

Nick turned away. The ostler had now abandoned his search for a suitable horse and was heading over to a new man who had entered the stables: Ward Dixon.

'A horse,' Ward snapped. 'And quickly.'

Over at the other end of the stable, Kyle snorted a laugh.

'Correction,' he said. 'I guess the three of us are riding together.'

CHAPTER 3

Doctor Weaver raised his hands and took a slow pace backwards.

'Don't threaten me, Chuck,' he said. 'I'm all that stands between this town and oblivion.'

'According to you,' Chuck Ellison said, 'the only reason we're facing oblivion is down to me and Frank.'

Weaver firmed his jaw, clearly unwilling to offer an apology. Lincoln stepped forward.

'I'm not standing for threats either,' he said.

Chuck gave him a brief glance. 'And who are you?'

'I'm the law here now and I'm helping Weaver save this town. Any man holding a gun on him will join my other prisoner in jail.'

For several moments the brothers stared at him, but when Lincoln resolutely returned their gazes Frank backed away for a step and Chuck lowered his rifle slightly. They shot worried glances at each other, possibly more from the thought of sharing a cell with someone than because a lawman was in town.

'We didn't mean no harm, lawman,' Chuck said.

'But we will do,' Frank said with more truculence than his brother had displayed as he pointed at Weaver, 'if you don't stop him spreading rumours.'

Seeing that the brothers were now backing down, Lincoln gestured for Weaver to join him in moving away. When this encouraged the two men to head back to their house, while still muttering to each other, the marshal and the doctor returned to town.

They said nothing until they reached the main drag, although Weaver had a firm-set jaw, as if the argument had irritated him more than he was trying to show.

'So those two are more annoyed than most that the death started there?' Lincoln said.

'The Ellison brothers have managed the wells for ten years without mishap, but people won't forget this. One day soon we'll heal. Then the recriminations will start and the Ellisons will be on the receiving end of most of them.'

'So that's the situation in town you wanted me see?'

'It's a part of it, the easiest part.' Weaver pointed, taking in the four compass points. 'Hope Wells runs east to west and every direction has problems. You came in from the east. With Hope Ridge to the south and west and the creek to the north, there's nothing but plains that way and that means it's the route that's the hardest to patrol and keep people away.'

Lincoln winced. 'I'd already encountered that problem.'

'To the west are the Ellison brothers and to the north and south are two blocks of buildings; both have plenty of problems. To the north are most of the saloons and hotels. When this broke out everyone there banded together to create their own cordon like the one outside town. Nobody goes in or out. I understand it's keeping the disease at bay.'

Lincoln looked to the indicated road. He could see only the first building and from memory he hadn't seen anyone on that road when he'd passed earlier.

'I can appreciate what they're doing. I'll talk with them and see how they're faring.'

'You didn't listen to me. Nobody goes in or out and that includes you. If you risk it, don't expect me to patch up the holes they'll bore in you. The water Rocky Bar ferries in is the key to survival, but they're refusing to trust anyone but themselves. They're living on whiskey and beer. It don't help them keep a sociable disposition.'

Lincoln nodded, then looked to the south.

'And the other way?'

'That way is hell on earth. The sick are there.' Weaver sighed. 'I've spent enough time showing you round. I need to get back to them.'

Weaver considered Lincoln with tired eyes. Then, with a weary air, he plodded towards the junction and the road that led to that side of town.

Lincoln hurried on to walk with him. 'I'm obliged

for your help. Now tell me what I can do to help.'

Weaver raised a hand, beckoning him to stay back.

'Patrol the main drag, keep people indoors, deal with the Ellisons, be friendly with the north side folk, and keep the peace. Leave the sick to me.'

Bearing in mind the massive problems Weaver faced, those tasks didn't sound enough. Lincoln was about to remonstrate with him, but a woman appeared at the corner. She was wringing her hands and sporting a worried look that said someone needed him.

Lincoln patted Weaver on the back and wished him well. He dallied for long enough to see Weaver speak with the woman, then lower his head and began to walk with her to the south side of town. Then he walked back to the law office.

On the boardwalk he took a last look around the deserted road, noting that after the animated activity of the last hour it had now returned to the same abandoned appearance that it'd had when he'd arrived. He walked inside, but a few paces in from the door he came to a sudden halt.

The cell door was swinging open. Marvin Sewell had gone. And so had the stolen money.

The mismatched group of three men rode out of Rocky Bar heading east and back along the route the stage had taken to enter town. Nick reckoned this subterfuge was essential and the other two men had agreed, not that Ward was any more communicative than when they'd travelled together on the stage.

Four miles out of town Nick had reason to be pleased he'd taken a cautious attitude. They were being followed.

He urged the others to maintain a calm, unhurried pace and to avoid looking back. They followed his orders and when several miles on they crested a rise letting them look back without drawing attention on themselves, Nick noted that the pursuers had drawn back.

At the bottom of the rise was the creek that circled around Rocky Bar and Hope Wells, so they took the opportunity to rest up for a while.

It was now late afternoon. To reach Hope Wells by sundown they would need to hurry. As the townsfolk had created a protective cordon around the town, which they would have to breach, Nick considered his options. They didn't seem promising.

'Even if those riders have stopped following us,' he said, 'we won't be able to get there while the light holds. I suggest we camp here tonight.'

Kyle frowned, but after a glance at the sun he agreed. Ward shook his head.

'We should move on,' he said, 'and use the cover of darkness.'

'I don't know the area well enough to lead us in.'

'I do. So I reckon this group needs a new leader.'

Nick shrugged. 'I've never claimed I'm the leader, and this isn't a group. I decided to go to Hope Wells. You two joined me.'

'No matter, staying together with me in charge will be better than three men blundering around on

24

their own.'

'I don't have a problem riding with Kyle. He can stay with me.' Nick glanced at Kyle, who nodded. 'You can take your own chances, without having to put up with me leading you.'

The argumentative Ward muttered to himself, then voiced more complaints, but Nick had made his view clear and Ward couldn't find a way to back down without losing face. Presently he prepared to move out, mumbling to himself with typical bad grace.

Nick ignored him while he busied himself by collecting kindling for a fire. Nobody spoke again until Ward was riding away.

'You reckon he'll get through?' Kyle said.

'If he knows the area, he might.' Nick winked, then opened his hands and let the kindling drop to the ground. 'So I reckon we keep an eye on him.'

'But I thought you said. . . .' Kyle sighed. 'You want him to get caught and draw the cordon?'

Nick said nothing else as from the corner of his eye he watched Ward ride along beside the creek. When he'd disappeared from view he hurried to the top of the rise and looked back towards town. Their followers had gone, so in short order he and Kyle mounted up.

They rode beside the water at a steady pace for five miles until Nick saw that Ward's tracks cut across the plains.

With a hand to his brow he considered the terrain. Ahead was the distant Hope Ridge which, despite Nick's limited knowledge of the area he knew skirted around Hope Wells. Nearer at hand low scrub covered the flat ground. After a few moments he picked out the distant speck that was Ward.

As the lowering sun was behind them, Ward wouldn't be able to see him and Kyle easily, so they speeded up. They halved the gap, then slowed to maintain their distance.

Nick could discern Ward's form. He showed no sign that he knew he was being followed. Only when he started climbing the ridge did Nick and Kyle seek cover in a depression, from where they watched Ward make his way from side to side as he gained height, until he disappeared into a gully. They followed.

When they reached the point where they'd lost sight of Ward they rode more cautiously, but as the sun was now setting they couldn't move too slowly. A sharp top to the ridge was ahead and they climbed towards it, eventually coming out on the edge of a sheer drop to the plains beyond.

They dismounted and dropped to their knees to crawl as close to the edge as they dared. Below was mainly flat and featureless ground, but in the gathering gloom was their target, the town about five miles away.

Nick stared at the buildings. They appeared as a dark smudge, and he tried to imagine what it would be like to be there. He wondered whether anyone was still alive. He sniffed and smelt something, his overactive imagination letting him identify it as the reek of death. With a shiver he looked to the terrain that lay between them and Hope Wells.

26

He couldn't see their quarry, but when he looked along the ridge he saw the route he must have taken, skirting along the top, then crossing back and forth to get down to ground level. He edged forward, seeking a sighting, then smiled and patted Kyle's shoulder.

'He's been captured,' Nick said. He pointed down, inviting Kyle to see for himself.

They watched Ward and the four men who had surrounded him. A discussion ensued, and to Nick's surprise it appeared to be amicable.

'The way Ward went is the only way I can see to get down,' Kyle said. He winced. 'And it looks as if they're coming back up here.'

Nick watched the group; he could see that they were indeed climbing back up to the top. He touched Kyle's shoulder and pointed to their horses. Doubled over, they sneaked away, standing up only when they were away from the edge. They hurried to their mounts.

They were twenty paces away when four men raised themselves and stood in their way. They skidded to a halt.

'You're not going nowhere,' one man said, his drawn six-shooter aimed at Nick.

'Hope Ridge,' the second man said, training his gun on Kyle while gesturing in a circle to indicate the terrain, 'is as close as anyone now gets to Hope Wells. We've got a new man in charge and he's reinforced the quarantine. The limit is five miles away and no closer.'

'It has to be our choice, whether we want to go there.'

27

The man ignored him and glanced at the men who had rounded up Ward. Nick and Kyle stayed quiet as the riders climbed to the summit and then skirted the edge to reach them. Their captors' silence and their keen glances suggested that the new leader was approaching, so Nick kept quiet until he could speak to the man who could decide whether they were allowed to be foolish.

'So we got both of them?' one of the approaching men hollered.

'All three,' Nick said.

The riders glanced at each other. They snorted laughs, then drew to a halt, but Ward continued. He didn't ride with the air of a man who was now a captive, which warned Nick of the problem to come.

'There were always just the two men to capture,' Ward said, using a calmer tone than his previous argumentative one.

'You saying you deliberately led us into a trap?'

'Sure. It let me see what I'm up against and it tested out the resources I'll have at my disposal.' Ward dismounted and came up to them, looking them up and down with disdain. 'And the answer is not much from you and plenty on my side.'

'Your side?'

'I'm now in charge of the quarantine around Hope Wells.' Ward rested a foot on a rock and looked down at the distant town. He smiled. 'The people down there are desperate. That means there's money to be made. And I'm the man to collect it.'

CHAPTER 4

'No further,' a strident voice demanded, stopping Lincoln in his tracks.

Lincoln had tried to take a direct route down the centre of the road to the barred north side of town, but as Weaver had warned him, he'd got no further than the crossroads before someone had spotted him.

He could see nobody in the street, so he ran his gaze across the buildings until a glint of light caught his attention in the corner of a saloon window. The pane was broken and a rifle barrel protruded.

'I'm Marshal Lincoln Hawk. Who's made the mistake of turning a gun on a lawman?'

For long moments silence greeted his demand. Then a muffled conversation ensued in the saloon, culminating in another man striding out on to the boardwalk. He walked with difficulty and he had to put a hand to the wall to steady himself before he faced Lincoln, adding credence to Weaver's claim that the men here were living on liquor.

'I'm Shelby Mix,' he said, the words slurred. 'What do you want, lawman?'

'I don't answer questions when I have a gun on me.'

Shelby looked towards the window and gave a brief nod. The barrel slipped from view and the gun-toter moved into the window to watch.

'Nobody's threatening you now.'

Lincoln glanced along the length of the buildings. He had no doubt that others would be watching, but Shelby had done as he asked.

'Sheriff Bester is dead. So I'm the law in town now.'

'You may be, but that don't mean you'll take another step.'

Lincoln didn't reply immediately, lasting out the tense moment and making Shelby push himself upright and glare at him as he awaited his response. Then Lincoln took a long, deliberate pace forward before he assumed a casual posture by folding his arms.

'You don't tell a lawman where he goes.' He took another pace making Shelby tense and the man in the saloon raise his rifle. 'But this disease needs containing and so creating effective barriers like yours is the right thing to do.'

Lincoln took a pace backwards making Shelby sigh with relief.

'Obliged you see it my way, Marshal.'

'I'm not violating your boundaries because I choose not to, not because you told me not to.'

30

'Understood.'

'So keep vigilant. I came here to arrest the outlaw Marvin Sewell. He's loose in town. If you see him, tell me.'

'If we see him, you'll hear the gunfire. We'll dump the body at the junction for you to collect.'

Lincoln tipped his hat before heading away. Marvin wouldn't have known about how the town had been divided up and as the jailhouse was on the south side of the main drag, it was probable he had gone that way.

As he didn't judge Marvin to be resourceful enough to free himself, Lincoln considered the question of who had freed him. The most likely possibility was that Marvin had deliberately come to Hope Wells because he knew someone here who would hide him.

That meant Lincoln needed to visit the south side. He wrapped a kerchief over his mouth and began the task.

The next hour was more troubling than anything he'd ever experienced.

He found Doctor Weaver in the first building he explored. He was being aided by the woman he'd seen earlier, who introduced herself as Gail Campbell. They appeared to be close, but it was hard to tell in what capacity as they were both exhausted.

They were dealing with a man who had died in bed alone in a room above his mercantile. Apparently he was a respected and long-standing member of the community, but the disease had stripped him of dignity, making him die in his own

31

filth in a stinking room.

Lincoln found a blanket in the storeroom. They wrapped his emaciated corpse in it, then carried him out the back.

'Couldn't someone else other than you two care for him?' Lincoln asked when they reached the fresh air outside.

Weaver shook his head. 'He wasn't even sick when I looked in on him yesterday and he was still distributing food to whoever needed it.'

Gail followed them out.

'That's the trouble with the disease,' she said. 'It strikes quickly and usually fatally. Within hours of falling ill you can be dead.'

Lincoln's heart beat faster, but he forced himself to keep calm and remember that he felt fine.

'We have to bury him quickly, then,' he said.

Weaver gave a forlorn smile, then pointed. Lincoln craned his neck as he moved forward until he saw what Weaver was indicating. He winced.

A burial detail was already working.

They were digging a shallow grave and throwing the earth aside. Mounds to the side showed that with the sun now lowering this had been a long day in which they'd dug many holes.

'We take the first free hole,' Weaver said.

'Doesn't it matter whose hole gets used?' Lincoln asked as they moved on. When Weaver furrowed his brow in confusion he continued. 'They were digging for someone and they didn't know this man would die.'

Weaver sighed. 'They're always digging. They start at sunup and work until sundown. The only certainty here is that someone will die. So they dig, someone dies, we bury them.'

Lincoln could think of nothing to say to that grim summation of the situation, but when he reached the latest hole he saw that it was even grimmer than he'd feared. To the right the line of mounds stretched away in an arc almost to the back of the law office. For over a hundred yards bodies had been placed ten feet apart and so there had to be around thirty people buried here.

Worse, the diggers were now doubling back to the law office, so the space would provide graves for at least another thirty. They'd already moved on to starting the next hole, the burial of the merchant not slowing them for even a moment.

'You expect all this space to be filled?' Lincoln murmured.

'This and more,' Weaver said, putting his end of the rolled-up blanket down beside the hole. 'They're digging while they still have the strength.'

Without ceremony Lincoln helped Weaver roll the body into the hole. Then, while Gail lowered her head and murmured a few words, Weaver found a spare shovel and covered the body with a layer of dirt, leaving the rest of the task to the diggers.

Lincoln cast a forlorn glance at the two men, not envying them their grim duty, then joined Weaver and Gail on their patrol. It turned out that neither of them had seen Marvin Sewell and they were too tired to care about Lincoln's problem.

After visiting the buildings on one side of the road Lincoln accepted the reason for their apathy.

They found two more bodies, including the town mayor who had been healthy only a few hours ago. They also found three more people who would be dead come sunup and whom Weaver could do nothing for other than to provide reassurance.

His greatest distress came from a sick member of a family that had so far avoided the disease. He gave them instructions for caring, using a monotone voice that showed how many times he had said this litany.

It was also clearly one that didn't work.

When they reached the end of the road and turned to go back up the other side, Lincoln found himself drawing back, unwilling to go on.

'You were right,' he said. 'This is hell on earth.'

'We've finished with the healthier side of the road,' Weaver said in a heavy tone. 'What's to come is worse.'

Lincoln lowered his head, feeling nauseated. When he'd taken a few deep breaths to regain his composure he decided to try another tactic to find Marvin. He stopped and faced the buildings they had yet to visit.

'Marvin Sewell,' he hollered, 'you must know now that you had a greater chance of survival in the jailhouse. Come out and I'll arrest you. Stay where you are and you'll die.'

Lincoln reckoned that at best this might worry Marvin into making a mistake, but to his surprise the door to a building fifty yards further on opened and Marvin paced out into the road. He had the saddle-bag of money draped over his left shoulder and dangling from his right hand was a six-shooter.

He stopped in the middle of the road and swung round to face Lincoln.

'I choose the third option,' he said. 'You die.'

'What're you going to do with us?' Kyle asked, fright widening his eyes.

Ward sneered with undisguised contempt at his scared behaviour, then moved on to stand before Nick.

'Are you going to beg too?' he asked.

'Just keep your hands off the kid,' Nick muttered.

'You're in no position to make threats.' Ward gestured to his men then back down the other side of the ridge. 'Take them to the creek.'

Everyone scurried to do his bidding. They were frisked for weapons. Then their belongings were searched. Nick had a six-shooter in his saddle-bag. Kyle was unarmed.

Then they were bundled away to their horses and led back down the slope taking them away from their planned destination. Ward sent half his number off to patrol the ridge and cordon leaving himself to take charge of taking them away.

Despite Ward's boasts and threatening attitude Nick reckoned he would still do nothing more than leave them by the water with stern warnings to stay away. In case he had a more sinister intent, as they rode along Nick sized up his escort.

Aside from Ward there were four men. Although they rode with confident airs they also frequently looked at Ward, perhaps hinting that they were unsure of the man who had now taken control of them.

Darkness had fallen when they reached the creek. Nick decided to force the situation, so when the group stopped he carried on riding.

'No further,' one man ordered from behind.

Nick waved a dismissive hand at him without looking back.

'There's no need to take us to Rocky Bar,' he said. 'We know the way.'

'We're not going there,' Ward said. He uttered a snort of laughter. 'But then again, neither are you.'

'Where are you taking us?' Kyle said, his voice small and scared.

Ward didn't reply until Nick drew his horse to a halt and turned.

'Just get off your horses,' he said, pointing, 'and go over there.'

Nick considered their captors. Kyle was still amongst them and he already looked so frightened he wouldn't need any encouragement to flee. But then he caught movement in the gloom. Three more men had been waiting for them by the creek.

Two men were standing, the third was sitting with his head bowed, his subdued demeanour being that of a prisoner. Nick reckoned he couldn't make a bolt for freedom and leave this man. So he did as ordered and with Kyle he dismounted.

When the prisoner noted them approaching, he stood to greet them with a wan half-smile.

'They catch you too?' he asked.

'Sure,' Nick said, joining him. 'This time.'

The man gave a brief nod, acknowledging that they thought alike. They exchanged names, Nick learning that he was Peter Campbell, but the pleasantries were cut short when Ward dismounted and stood before them.

'There won't be a next time,' he said.

'You only have to worry about the Hope Wells folk getting out,' Nick said. 'If people want to risk getting in, that's their decision.'

'That was how things used to be run, but an old friend saw the situation differently. He reckoned there was an opportunity here and he called me in to exploit it.'

'Where is he?'

'You ask too many questions for a dead man.' Ward glanced at the nearest man. 'Make sure their bodies float well out into the water.'

'Don't,' Peter shouted, darting forward for a pace before he was dragged back. 'I just want to get into town to be with my wife. She went there to help the sick. No matter what you men are trying to do here, you must understand that.'

Ward looked Peter up and down, then moved on to Kyle, who lowered his head. He stopped in front of Nick.

'So I have a newspaperman looking for a story, a

man looking for his wife, and a mystery man looking for something he won't reveal. There's nothing here to persuade me not to kill you.'

Nick could see no reason to avoid explaining himself. Talking might provide a distraction that would let him take on his captors.

'There's no mystery,' he said. 'I'm looking for Marvin Sewell.'

'Never heard of him.' Ward started to move away.

'And Brad Ellison.'

Ward flinched, his eyebrows rising in surprise.

'Why?'

'To kill them.'

For long moments Ward considered him. Then he spread his hands.

'Then you should have told me that earlier. Any enemy of Brad's is a friend of mine.'

CHAPTER 5

'You're no fast draw, gunslinger,' Lincoln said, eyeing Marvin Sewell.

'I don't need to be,' Marvin said with confidence as he settled his stance.

Lincoln had only rarely found himself in show-down situations where he had to rely purely on the speed with which he could draw. But luckily he had been apprised of his opponent's abilities. He was just an opportunistic thief with a history of committing minor misdemeanours.

Except that Marvin was smirking as he waited for Lincoln to make his move. He shouldn't be that assured.

Lincoln flicked his gaze to the building in which Marvin had been hiding. In an upstairs window gun-metal caught a stray beam of light, confirming that the marshal had been right to be cautious.

Lincoln leapt to the left, saving himself from a slug that kicked dirt at his feet. He landed on his side, rolled, then came to rest on his front. Marvin made use of the distraction to take flight, so Lincoln threw his hand to his holster, then picked out the man in the window.

His shot shattered the remaining shards of glass, but the man still fired back. The slug whined, making Lincoln's hat jerk to one side as the bullet almost delivered a fatal blow, but Lincoln made the man pay for attempting such a difficult shot. He aimed at his chest and thudded a slug into him.

The man cried out, his gun falling from his slackening fingers, to skitter down the boardwalk canopy. The man followed it. He tumbled forward, hitting the roof with a shoulder, then skidding down to the ground.

Before he'd hit the hardpan Lincoln was gaining his feet to follow Marvin, who had now reached the corner and was running out on to the main drag. Lincoln followed.

By the time Marvin had disappeared from view around the corner Lincoln was pounding across the ground. He reached the corner twenty seconds after Marvin and saw he'd chosen the one route that guaranteed failure. He was running to the road that led to the north side.

Lincoln slowed, letting Marvin get ahead and so making him face the trouble alone. When Marvin rounded the corner he glanced over his shoulder and saw that he was moving away from Lincoln. He grinned before he went out of view.

Several seconds passed. Then the shooting started. Marvin cried out, demanding that the shooters stop, and when Lincoln, having made steady progress down the road, was able to size up the situation, he saw that Marvin had got no further than he himself had earlier. He was standing thirty yards from the saloon with his arms thrust high.

Not only was a man holding a gun on him from the saloon, but others had come out of hiding on the other side of the road to keep him covered.

'No further,' Shelby said, edging out from the saloon. 'Nobody enters the north side.'

'I'm no trouble,' Marvin shouted. 'I've just arrived and I've stayed away from the sick people.'

'That's a good plan and it's one we're following too.' Shelby looked past Marvin at Lincoln. 'And luckily the lawman's here to drag your body away, so we don't have to touch you.'

Marvin looked at Lincoln as he stopped at the end of the road. Lincoln shook his head, telling him that retreat would lead to his immediate arrest. Marvin considered the men holding a gun on him.

His shoulders slumped as he appeared to accept he was outnumbered, but to Lincoln's surprise he took a half-pace towards the saloon.

'That's a foolish move,' Lincoln urged. 'Keep it up and you won't live for long enough to get arrested.'

Marvin continued to use a sidling motion with his hands raised. After another two paces a gunshot tore into the ground beside his feet. Marvin took another pace and a second shot thudded into the hardpan so close to his boot it made him raise his foot and glance at it.

41

'One more pace,' Shelby said, 'and we'll blast your toes off.'

Marvin stomped his feet to the ground in a show of not going any further. Then, moving slowly while keeping his hands away from his holster, he unhooked the saddle-bag from his shoulder.

'I have money,' he said. 'Enough to buy safety.'

Shelby said nothing. Marvin opened the bag. He drew out a handful of bills and waved them. This gathered Shelby's attention, but he still shook his head.

'Nobody can buy their way in here. Death isn't worth it.'

His words might have been defiant but Shelby edged to the end of the boardwalk so he could see the money more clearly. Heartened, Marvin withdrew a second handful.

'I've been told,' he said, 'that once you catch this disease you die quickly. For a man as healthy looking as me, there must be an alternative.'

Shelby shuffled from side to side while rubbing his jaw. He glanced at the various gunmen on the road. Most of them returned slight nods. In a gruff voice he provided his verdict.

'There must,' he said.

Marvin slapped the bills back into the bag, then cast a triumphant glance at Lincoln, who couldn't contain himself any longer. He started pacing down the road.

'You can't protect my prisoner,' he shouted. 'He was hiding out on the south side of town.'

42

'I'll take precautions,' Shelby said, looking along the road at the various buildings as he turned to the practicalities. 'I'll keep him separate until I'm sure he's not going to fall ill.'

'I didn't mean that,' Lincoln said, shaking a fist. 'You refused me access because you had a rigid protection policy to enforce. I agreed with you. But where are your principles now if you let an outlaw in for money?'

Shelby frowned, leaving Marvin to shout his defiance.

'Run along, lawman,' he gloated. 'You can't have me now.'

Lincoln stopped and pointed a firm finger at him.

'Shelby can't protect you from me, and your money won't protect you from the disease.'

Lincoln looked in turn at each man on the road. Then he headed back to the main drag to continue helping Weaver with his grim duties. As he strode away he didn't look back to see what Shelby did with Marvin.

His irritation lessened when he rejoined the doctor and saw that he was dealing with the aftermath of the earlier gunfight. He was wrapping the shot man up in a blanket, but on seeing Lincoln approaching he stood back to let him examine the body.

'It's Eddie Bryce,' he said. 'He's the first healthy person to die here in a while.'

'The name doesn't mean anything,' Lincoln said. He considered Weaver's frown. 'But I figure you're not surprised to find he broke Marvin out of jail.'

'Sure not. Back in the days when this town had normal problems to deal with, Eddie was a trouble-maker, and his chief associate was the third and worst of the Ellison brothers, Brad.'

'The men who spread the plague.' Lincoln faced west and the wells. 'I'll give them time to hear about what happened here and stew over it. Then I'll pay these brothers a longer visit.'

'Is he convinced?' Kyle asked.

'Yeah,' Nick said, joining him and Peter at the bar. 'But I have news that'll surprise you. We're working for Ward now in patrolling the cordon.'

As Nick reached for a glass Peter slammed a fist on the bar, making the glass fall over and roll away from his hand.

'I'll never work for him,' he muttered. 'You're on your own.'

'Relax,' Nick said, rescuing the glass before it fell off the bar. 'I didn't try to persuade him to accept you. He believed you when you said you hated Brad Ellison too, and that was good enough for him. But we're newcomers and it didn't take much for me to talk him into accepting us.'

'I'm pleased for you.' Peter pushed himself away from the bar, but he stopped beside Nick. 'You saved my life back there and I'm grateful, but don't get in my way when I next try to reach Hope Wells.'

Peter turned away, but Nick slapped a hand on his shoulder, halting him. Peter shook the hand off and

44

spun round. Anger darkened his eyes, but when Nick returned his gaze with an amused smile tugging at the corners of his lips, he relaxed his hunched shoulders.

'Quit getting so worked up and join us.' Nick gestured to the bar. 'I'll explain.'

Peter did as requested, although he continued to look at Nick oddly, as did Kyle.

'I hope,' Kyle said, 'that you have some kind of ruse in mind.'

'I have,' Nick said, evoking two relieved sighs. 'Ward's muscled in on operations here quickly and he needs help to reinforce his position. I offered it.'

'That's good work, but it doesn't mean we'll be able to reach Hope Wells.'

'We can come and go around the cordon. So we have a better chance than it looked like we'd get earlier.'

Kyle nodded, but Peter was still frowning.

'That doesn't help me,' he said.

'It might.' Nick offered a smile. 'If you trust me.'

CHAPTER 6

Patrolling the cordon was more boring than Nick had expected.

His hectic day yesterday had given him the impression that streams of people were attempting to reach or leave Hope Wells. But from high up on Hope Ridge he and Kyle saw nobody and they had such a good view of the plains that anyone approaching from the creek would be easily visible, showing why they had been apprehended quickly yesterday.

The view in the opposite direction was equally clear and equally unmarred by activity. Either the Hope Wells folk were displaying admirable fortitude in their decision to sit the situation out, or they were too ill to leave.

This didn't change Nick's determination that he would go there when he was sure of success, and Kyle agreed.

Around noon two surly men relieved them, both of whom had been amongst the group that had been prepared to kill them last night. They then carried out a roving brief in which they took in the perimeter of the cordon. This proved to be five miles out of town following a rough circle that incorporated several rocky landmarks.

At each landmark a group of men was on lookout and each time they reported to each other that nothing was amiss. When they reached a point facing the ridge and the town, the gap between the gunmen was the widest they'd come across so far, but Nick still reckoned that anyone heading to town would be seen. There were rocks and depressions, but not enough for anyone to cover any great distance unseen.

'This won't be easy,' Kyle said, matching Nick's thoughts.

'We just have to bide our time,' Nick said as they set off on the return journey. 'A chance is sure to come our way soon.'

Kyle nodded, after which they reverted to silence.

It was late afternoon when, after an uneventful patrol, they approached the ridge.

An open wagon and several riders had drawn up. Nick hadn't seen these men before. They were milling around, clearly waiting for someone, although they looked at the patrollers with disinterest suggesting it wasn't them.

The sight made Kyle fidget in the saddle. After peering at the men and presumably also deciding that he didn't recognize them, he took a deep breath. Then, after a sideways glance at Nick, he asked him the question he had been expecting since yesterday.

'Who are Marvin Sewell and Brad Ellison?'

'That sure is a difficult question,' Nick said, providing the answer he'd prepared beforehand, 'for a man to give to a correspondent of the *North Town Times.*'

Kyle didn't reply immediately. When he did his voice was almost too low to be heard over the steady clop of hoofs.

'I can understand why you might not want to talk to me, but what if I were to tell you a secret?'

Nick was minded to let the young man keep his secret, but he could tell that revealing it was important to him.

'Speak,' he said.

'I'm not a correspondent.' This revelation made Nick swirl round in the saddle to face him, but in response Kyle merely shrugged. 'Well, I'm not exactly a correspondent yet.'

'But this story might help?'

'You understand.' Kyle took a deep breath. 'I do work at the *North Town Times*, but I only swept up while trying to learn the business. Sadly all I learnt was how to brush away dirt. So I asked what I had to do to become a correspondent. Come up with a big story, I was told. So I got on the stage and headed to the nearest town that didn't have a correspondent already. And there is a story here and I intend to report on it.'

Nick nodded. 'We're dealing with dangerous men,

so do you know how to defend yourself?'

'I'm not armed.' Kyle smiled. 'But I know how to wield a brush.'

Nick laughed. Kyle had started to join in when gunfire tore out ahead.

The riders beside the wagon jerked their horses around in a circle searching for the source of the shooting, but before they could locate it, two men tumbled from their mounts.

This at least let the others identify the spot on the ridge where the shooters were. The wagon driver moved the wagon on, aiming to place it sideways to the ridge and give the rest cover. He completed the operation, but then he stood up straight with a hand clutching his chest and keeled over, to fall to the ground.

The remaining men jumped down from their horses and hurried into hiding behind the wagon leaving Nick and Kyle with a problem.

'Help them or not?' Nick asked.

'We're unarmed,' Kyle said. 'About the only thing we can do is get ourselves killed, and besides, we don't know who these people are.'

Nick looked along the ridge, searching for the position of the shooters. He couldn't see them, but there was a wide gap between the ridge and the wagon and that gave him an idea.

'I reckon that's a group of townsfolk trying to break out,' he said. 'We should help them move on back to the safety of town.'

'It's a good idea, but how?'

Nick pointed, indicating a route they could take to reach the wagon then move it back towards Hope Wells. Kyle gave him a long look that acknowledged how reckless the plan was, but he didn't argue. So they moved on, skirting away from the ridge to stay out of gunfire range while moving in towards the wagon.

This let them see the men hiding behind the wagon, who followed their progress.

'We're aiming to help you get back!' Nick hollered.

His offer made the men glance at each other and shrug, but they didn't turn guns on them. So when Nick and Kyle were directly behind the wagon, they stopped to pick their moment to make their move.

The cowering men watched them, but while their attention was elsewhere the shooters on the ridge made their own move. Two groups of riders hurtled into view, seeking to outflank the wagon and take them on either side.

'Watch out!' Kyle shouted, raising himself in the saddle and pointing, but he was already too late. The attackers had drawn level with the wagon.

As the riders came in on either side the defenders darted to the left and right, searching for the best way to repel the attack. They failed. Three men went down in the first volley of lead, leaving only two men standing.

One of these men tried to run to safety. He pounded across the ground towards Nick and Kyle, but several gunshots to the back made him go down.

The second man scurried into temporary safety beneath the wagon, taking himself out of Nick's view, but within moments the riders closed on the wagon and they joined forces to blast down at him.

Then the shooters rode around the wagon, checking that they'd dispatched everyone before they faced Nick and Kyle. Behind the wagon Ward came into view, riding steadily on and with his gaze set beyond the wagon at them.

'Run or brazen this out?' Nick asked.

'I doubt we could escape,' Kyle said. 'But I reckon if Ward had wanted us dead, he'd have killed us last night.'

With this assessment not cheering either man, they moved on. The aftermath of the massacre became evident. The men with the wagon had been holed repeatedly. Ward's men were dragging them together, showing no distaste at handling plague folk from Hope Wells, as Nick had expected.

He saw the reason why when they rode past the man who had run towards them. The man wasn't from Hope Wells. He was one of the men from Rocky Bar who had remonstrated with Ward yesterday. In a shocking moment of clarity Nick understood the reason for the attack.

Ward wasn't keeping the plague folk within the cordon; he was asserting his authority over the cordon and wiping out those who didn't agree with his plans. Nick glanced at Kyle and the sorry look he returned confirmed that he had reached the same conclusion.

51

'Quiet around the rest of the cordon?' Ward said with mock lightness when they drew up before him. He licked his lips, clearly relishing their reactions.

'We haven't seen anyone approaching town or leaving,' Nick said. He glanced at the heaped bodies, then firmed his jaw to avoid showing his distaste. 'Does this mean you've eliminated all your enemies?'

'Hope so,' Ward said, looking from one man to the other. 'And you two certainly helped with your distraction.'

As Ward was baiting them, Nick sought to change the subject by pointing at the wagon. It was loaded down with four large barrels. They hadn't been holed, but one was leaking water with a steady drip.

'That's a lot of water for our small group.'

'It's not for us. It's generous aid for the distressed townsfolk of Hope Wells.'

Ward chuckled and after he had looked at the other men they joined in, confirming that generosity was the last thing on his mind.

'Surely the one thing that town has is water?'

'Yeah, but the problem is their wells are contaminated. They need a fresh supply from the creek every day to keep the plague under control. So they come to the perimeter to beg for water.'

Nick noted the smirks everyone was casting at the others.

'And these men were going to give the townsfolk what they want until you stopped them?'

'Almost right. These men were planning to hand over the water for free. I want fifty dollars a barrel.'

Ward glanced around his men, all of whom nodded approvingly before he cast a significant look at the bodies.

'Fifty dollars is a fair price,' Nick said, forcing out the words he had to say to avoid meeting the same fate as the dead men. 'But the men who carry out the transfer would have to come from your most trusted men.'

'Or from the most expendable.' Ward laughed. 'But you're right. Anyone who went would either be trusted, or would earn my trust.'

Nick didn't think it was worth continuing the conversation when Ward had clearly made up his mind to use this unpleasant task to test their loyalty. As Kyle curled his lip conveying a mixture of worry and disgust, Nick dismounted and headed to the water wagon.

'When will the water be picked up?' he asked when he was sitting on the seat with Kyle beside him.

'Head for town at sundown. The deal's been done and they'll see you coming. Just don't get too close.'

Nick felt an urge to get away from the bodies quickly, so, with a glance at the lowering sun, he moved the wagon on so as to ride alongside the ridge.

Behind them, the men chortled and shouted unhelpful advice after them about how to avoid catching the plague. Nick kept the wagon going for several hundred yards before Kyle looked at him.

'I knew Ward would seize control and then profit out of this situation,' Kyle said, 'but seeing it happen and helping him do it doesn't make me feel good.'

'I'm angry too.' Nick raised himself to look ahead at a mound that spread out from the end of the ridge on to the plains. 'But perhaps we can use this situation to our advantage. If you're thirsty, we could stop here and I could tell you my secret.'

'Secret?' Kyle furrowed his brow but on seeing that Nick was forcing a smile he returned a thin smile of his own. 'I'd like to hear about Marvin Sewell and Brad Ellison, but I'm not thirsty.'

'You are,' Nick insisted. 'Use the leaky barrel and leave the lid off.' He gave Kyle a long look until he returned a slow nod as an understanding of Nick's intention hit him. Then Nick swung the wagon towards the mound.

When they'd stopped Kyle clambered into the back of the wagon. While he struggled to remove the top from the barrel Nick resisted the urge to look along the ridge to see whether Ward was watching them. Instead, he adopted the demeanour of a man wasting time before making the rendezvous by leaning back in his seat and drawing his hat down over his eyes.

'Ward's men have split up,' Kyle reported when he returned, wiping his mouth. 'Half are heading on to the plains with the bodies and the rest are climbing the ridge. None of them was paying us much attention.'

'Good, but in case they do, look relaxed.'

'That's hard.' Kyle sighed. 'But perhaps that secret might take my mind off things.'

54

'It won't, because Brad Ellison is a nasty piece of work. But my problem is with Marvin Sewell, my sister's no-good husband. He'd been in prison and she never wanted to see him again. But he served his time and returned, claiming to be a changed man. She gave him a second chance then and begged me to do the same. So I employed him at the White Ridge depot. He repaid me by stealing five hundred dollars. He went west and I reckoned he was planning to meet up with his old cellmate Brad.'

'Why?'

'Apparently he owed him money. I reckon he stole to repay the debt.'

'And when you catch up with them?'

'I'll politely ask for the money back.' Nick smiled and when Kyle returned that smile, he shrugged. 'But I promised my sister I'd help Marvin out of this mess, so this is his very last chance. If he sides with me against Brad, I'll forgive him. Otherwise. . . .'

Kyle nodded. Then both men glanced at the setting sun.

'I haven't seen anything untoward,' Kyle said, 'but while you were talking I heard a noise in the back of the wagon.'

'In that case it's time to go.'

Nick moved off and, mindful of the unwelcome task ahead of them, both men remained silent. They headed for the nearest landmark of a sentinel boulder where three gunmen waved them on.

After another 400 yards the town appeared ahead and a further hundred yards on Nick saw an open wagon approaching. As they had travelled into a depression that hid them from the gunmen he stopped. Then he manoeuvred the wagon into a position where the barrels could be easily rolled down to a dip and then back up on to the townsfolk's wagon.

When the other wagon stopped fifty yards away, the driver introduced himself as Doctor Weaver.

'That's a good place to leave the barrels,' he shouted. 'I can deal with them from there.'

'It's not as simple as that,' Nick shouted. 'We need something from you first.'

'I have it, and I hope Ward Dixon chokes on it.'

With a reluctant air Weaver took a bag from the back of the wagon and jumped down from the seat. He took several paces and then with an angry oath, he launched the bag towards them. The bag fell ten yards short, but with this begrudging acceptance of the deal, Nick nudged Kyle.

'Ask your questions,' he said, 'while I deal with the barrels.'

'Obliged,' Kyle said. He moved off to stand beside the bag.

While he shouted questions to Weaver, and received short answers, Nick rolled the barrels off the wagon. He managed to move the first three easily, but the last one required more manoeuvring and effort.

When he paused to gather his breath he listened to the questioning and gathered that after at first being uncooperative, the possibility of the town's story becoming known had enthused Weaver.

Nick slid the last barrel down the backboard on to the soft dirt. After that he checked each barrel by raising the lid and looking inside.

The levels of water were high, cheering him as they hadn't lost much water in transit, but when he raised the fourth lid the leak had ensured that most of the water had gone. But he did receive a wink and a mouthed *thank you.*

Nick returned the wink, then leaned down.

'Best of luck in finding your wife,' he whispered.

Peter nodded. Nick replaced the lid, then joined Kyle. As his young associate was still asking questions, Nick looked in the bag. He riffled through it, then winced. There was only fifty dollars inside.

He waited until Kyle had stopped speaking, then waved the bag at Weaver.

'Ward said the agreement was for fifty dollars a barrel.'

'I won't pay two hundred dollars!' Weaver spluttered.

'I understand.' Nick pointed back towards the ridge. 'But there are some ruthless men back there.'

Weaver nodded, then lowered his tone to a less irritated level.

'If Ward is going after every cent we have, he'll find out how determined our people are.'

Nick spread his hands. 'I'm on your side. Look in the leaky barrel before you put it on your wagon and you'll see that. Don't risk taking Ward on and don't worry about the money this time. Take the water and pay him later.'

'Then I'm obliged, but I won't have the money later either. Hope Wells didn't have that sort of money when we were thriving. We're dying now.'

'But someone might have. Did Marvin Sewell come to town?'

'Yeah,' Weaver said using a guarded tone.

Nick breathed a sigh of relief. 'He came to see Brad Ellison to repay a debt. He has five hundred dollars of stolen money. If you can find it, use it.'

Weaver nodded. 'I'm obliged for what you're doing. Be careful.'

'Don't worry about us.' Nick mustered a tense smile. 'We can deal with Ward.'

CHAPTER 7

'At last,' Lincoln said as Weaver drew up the water wagon loaded with barrels. His voice emerged as a pained croak as he'd not drunk anything since arriving in town yesterday.

He had decided against using the policy Shelby's group had employed of living on liquor, but that decision had weighed heavily on him as his second day in town had dragged on.

Earlier today he'd gone to see the Ellison brothers to see what part they'd played in Marvin Sewell's activities, but they'd gone to ground. He had resisted the urge to search for them and instead he had conserved his strength by sitting outside the law office and letting the day drift by.

Doctor Weaver and Gail Campbell had also had a less fraught day and they'd been able to rest, but sadly that was only because they now had fewer people to care for. The doctor hoped that the fresh water would improve the town's fortunes, so Lincoln was surprised to see that when Weaver jumped down from the wagon he was frowning.

'We've got plenty of problems,' he reported. 'But for now we should just worry about getting the water to those who need it.'

'Will four barrels be enough?'

'It'll have to be, and there's only three.' Weaver reached over the side of the wagon and patted a barrel. A hollow thud sounded. 'You can come out now.'

A pained muttering sounded. Then with a thump the lid went flying into the air. Two hands appeared as a man tried to prise himself out.

'What the. . . ?' Lincoln murmured before he got over his surprise and jumped up on to the back to help him out.

'I'm Peter,' the man said as he stumbled round on the spot, bent over.

Lincoln waited for an explanation, and when Peter had righted his stooped posture he got his answer. Gail flinched, then stared up at him, her mouth opening wide in surprise.

'You came,' she murmured.

'For my wife, of course I did,' Peter said. He jumped down from the wagon to stand before her.

'I didn't want you to risk yourself,' she said backing away for a pace and shaking her head.

'And I didn't want you to risk yourself, but you still came here.'

'I had to. Doctor Weaver needed me.'

Peter narrowed his eyes. With his jaw set firm he paced up to Weaver.

'That's all I needed to hear,' he muttered. Then he drew back his fist and delivered a swiping round-armed punch to Weaver's jaw that sent the doctor reeling.

'Why?' Weaver murmured when he'd slid to a halt on his rump.

'You know why.' Peter stood over him with his fist drawn back while Weaver felt his jaw. 'Now get up so I can knock you down again.'

Lincoln got over his surprise at the same time as Gail did and they both rushed to the two men. Gail grabbed her husband's arm while Lincoln put himself between Peter and Weaver.

'Enough,' he said.

Peter glanced at Lincoln's star. 'This isn't a matter for no lawman. This is between Weaver and me.'

'And me,' Gail screeched, struggling and failing to drag him away. 'It's not what you think. He's never touched me.'

'He sure used to do plenty of touching when he worked in Rocky Bar, and I can't see no other reason why you'd come to this hell-hole.'

'To save lives! That's what I do. His nurse died and he needed my help.'

For the first time since he'd attacked Weaver, Peter looked at her with affection. Something in her pleading eyes made his shoulders slump and he let her draw him away. Seeing his change of heart, Weaver raised a hand for Lincoln to pull him to his feet.

'And she's been invaluable, Peter,' he said. 'Many more people would have died if she hadn't joined me.'

His comment only served to inflame Peter again. He shook Gail's hand off him and advanced on Weaver, but the weary doctor was in no mood for a fight. He waved a dismissive hand at Peter and turned to the wagon.

'Don't turn your back on me,' Peter roared. He charged Weaver.

He covered three paces at a run until Lincoln moved to the side and caught him with a leading shoulder, knocking him aside. Peter tried to right himself but his foot landed on a damp spot beside the wagon and he went sprawling all his length.

Peter lay gathering his breath. Then with a slap of a fist against the ground he came up with his eyes blazing and his face red. The embarrassment of the tumble and the incorrect assumption he'd made about Weaver and Gail knocked all the sense from his mind. He picked out the nearest target – Lincoln – and charged him with his fists flailing.

Lincoln tried to dodge the punches but they came quickly and they were thrown with a frantic determination to inflict injury on someone. So Lincoln backed away, taking several blows to the body until he got his first opening. Then he thundered a pile-driver of a blow into Peter's guts.

Peter folded over the blow, coughing and holding his stomach. Lincoln didn't give him a chance to regain his strength; he delivered a swinging uppercut to his chin that stood him up straight. Then a straight jab to the nose toppled him.

Lincoln stood over Peter confirming that he'd

knocked the fight out of him. Peter was now more concerned with stemming the blood flow from his crushed nose and curling into a ball to avoid further blows. Lincoln turned to Gail.

'We can't fight amongst ourselves,' he said. 'So talk sense into him, or I'll knock it into him.'

Gail nodded and knelt beside her husband. She murmured comforting words that gradually made him relax, so, with the situation appearing resolved, Lincoln helped Weaver roll the first barrel down to the ground.

'Peter's wrong,' Weaver said when the barrel had come to rest.

In view of the dire situation that they faced, Lincoln hadn't spent any time considering why Gail was here, but he had noticed that Weaver and she were close, and he had reached the same conclusion as Peter. He shrugged.

'It's none of my business,' he said. 'Getting this water distributed is.'

Lincoln took the opportunity to drink from the barrel while Weaver looked around to check on the others. Peter was now sitting up and leaning back against a wheel while talking quietly to Gail. Both of them were nodding frequently as they reconciled their differences.

Lincoln couldn't help but notice that Weaver let his gaze linger on the couple and that the doctor ground his jaw until he noticed that Lincoln was looking at him. He swirled away from them in a guilty way then offered Lincoln a smile.

'We have a problem keeping the water coming,' he said. 'A man called Ward Dixon is now looking after the cordon. I paid him for this water, but it sounds as if that price will keep going up.'

'I thought I heard shooting. I'll deal with him.'

'You might get help from the two men who brought the water, Kyle Portman and Nick Mitchell.'

Lincoln nodded. 'Nick looked after the White Ridge depot. Marvin Sewell stole money that'd been entrusted to him.'

'And he's come to get it back, except he's worked out why Marvin fled here. Marvin was in debt to Brad Ellison.'

Lincoln slapped the side of the wagon in irritation.

'It always comes back to the Ellisons.' He moved to a spot where he could see the Ellisons' building beyond the edge of town. 'Deal with the water. It's time I dealt with them.'

Weaver cast a worried glance at Peter, then nodded.

'Gail and I can do that, if Peter will let us.'

Lincoln nodded, accepting the doctor's concern, and went over to the couple.

'Have you calmed down yet?' he asked, standing over Peter, who looked up with muted anger in his eyes, but when Gail urged him to reply he scowled and mustered a begrudging answer.

'No,' he said, 'but Gail's right. This isn't the time for arguments. I'll settle this with Weaver later.'

'In that case, I have a job for you that'll work off

your anger. I'm going after the Ellisons.'

'The good-for-nothing Ellisons!' Peter produced the first smile Lincoln had seen. 'Now why didn't you say that earlier?'

'Fifty dollars!' Ward muttered, waving the bills Nick had collected. 'Where's the rest?'

Nick folded his arms and cast his measured gaze around the circle of men. Behind them Hope Ridge presented a dark expanse against the rapidly darkening sky.

'You told Doctor Weaver you wanted fifty dollars in total,' he said, 'not fifty for every barrel.'

Ward smirked. 'It was a test of your initiative and commitment. You failed.'

'That was an impossible test. Weaver didn't have the money.'

'That means he's not desperate enough yet.'

Nick lowered his head, searching for another way to talk reason into the man, but to his surprise Kyle spoke up.

'But he will be soon,' he said. 'We told him to pay up the rest tomorrow, except tomorrow the price will go up again.'

Ward swung round to consider him. He laughed.

'That was my plan, kid.' He bowed with mock magnanimity. 'Get the money tomorrow and Weaver can still have his water.'

Neither Kyle nor Nick questioned this order and they quickly collected their horses. Having been on patrol all day, they left the night duty and headed back to Rocky Bar. Others were also returning to town but they made no effort to ride with them. Only when they were alone did Nick turn to Kyle.

'What's on your mind?' he asked.

'Same as yours,' Kyle said, 'that this is wrong and that we have to do something about it.'

'I didn't think correspondents got involved.'

'I'm not a correspondent.'

Nick laughed. 'And you won't get to be one unless we're careful. It's not certain that Weaver will be able to find Marvin or Brad and reclaim the stolen money, and even if he does that'll only delay a confrontation. I'm not getting the money back only to give it to Ward.'

'I don't reckon you'll have to. You probably didn't hear everything Doctor Weaver said, but a US marshal has followed Marvin Sewell to town. He won't accept being held to ransom.'

'So Marshal Lincoln Hawk's here too,' Nick mused. He smiled. 'If we could smuggle a man into town without the gunmen patrolling the cordon noticing, we should be able to smuggle a lawman out.'

CHAPTER 8

'How do you know Brad Ellison?' Lincoln asked when they reached the edge of town and were facing the wells.

'Everyone knows Brad,' Peter said. 'People borrow a few dollars off him and then he claims they owe him hundreds. He always collects, one way or the other, and since he came back from prison he's been even worse.'

Lincoln stopped in front of the fence that surrounded the wells.

'Understood. As you know the brothers, give me a few minutes then holler to get them outside.'

Lincoln patted his back, then hurried off along the side of the fence to reach the back of the building. Then he slipped through the bars and ran to the back corner. There he signalled to Peter, who hollered out for the Ellisons to come out.

Several minutes passed in which Peter shouted twice more before two of the brothers, Frank and Chuck, emerged, slouching and grumbling. They came towards the fence, but they stopped ten yards away from Peter, who showed subtlety for the first time by engaging them in animated conversation, which kept their attention and drew them closer.

Lincoln sidled along while keeping his back to the wall, then hurried around the corner and to the door. He slipped inside to find that the building enclosed an open space, half of it being used for business and the other half providing a crude home.

Along one wall barrels had been stocked beside an open wagon. Another wagon lay on its side. It was being repaired, although its rotting state suggested that this work had been going on for some time.

Against the opposite wall were rolled-up blankets, but not much else, showing that the brothers weren't exactly homemakers. The bigger problem was that Lincoln could see into all corners of the building and there was no sign of Brad.

Moving cautiously Lincoln slipped behind the barrels and walked along beside the wall. Nobody was hiding there, so he searched their belongings for anything to confirm that Brad was staying here.

'What you doing?' Chuck Ellison's harsh voice muttered behind him.

Lincoln took his time in stopping, making the point that he had a right to be here. Chuck was standing in the doorway with his brother Frank. Peter was loitering behind him, but he was watching both men in case of trouble.

'I'm looking for Brad.'

Both brothers winced before they masked their

reactions by coming inside.

'Whatever trouble he's in is his problem,' Chuck said, 'not ours.'

'That's a laudable attitude. So prove it. Tell me where he is and I'll leave.'

'He's not here. That's all we care about.'

'With Eddie Bryce?'

The brothers glanced at each other in a guilty manner so transparent that Lincoln had to bite his lip to avoid smiling. As their silence dragged on Peter followed them into the doorway, where he leaned against the side of the door and glared at them, adding to their discomfiture.

'He could be with him,' Frank said without much conviction.

Lincoln gave each man in turn a long stare.

'Is that so? Because you see the thing is, I'm surprised you haven't heard that I shot up Eddie yesterday. Brad wasn't with him. So either you didn't know that, or you're lying.'

Both men gulped showing that in truth it had been a bit of both.

'We can't help you, lawman,' Chuck said, not meeting his eye.

Peter took several long paces to stand at Chuck's shoulder.

'I've been through hell to get here,' he muttered into Chuck's right ear. 'I hid in one of your stinking barrels, beat up a man who might not have deserved it, then got beaten up myself. So I'm not in the mood for no messing around. Tell the marshal where he can find Brad.'

Chuck shrank away from him, then stammered a barely audible refusal, but Frank mustered a whispered comment.

'He's not here.'

Chuck rounded on his brother, but before he could remonstrate with him Peter pushed him aside and stalked up to Frank. He grabbed his vest front, hoisted him up, then walked him backwards and slammed his back to the wall.

'Where?' he muttered.

Lincoln moved over to stand at Peter's shoulder, reinforcing the demand. Frank cast him a worried glance, then looked to Chuck, who shook his head.

'Don't—' Chuck said, but he didn't get to finish his order before Peter thumped Frank in the stomach, blasting the air from his chest. Then he pressed him back against the wall again.

'I don't want to hear nothing but answers. I've had enough of this town and I'm waiting for the right moment to fight back. I reckon I'll start with you.'

Peter hurled back his fist and took a pace backwards to give himself room for a solid blow. His intention at last got through to Frank and he bleated out a cry of desperation.

'No!' he screeched. 'Don't hit me. Brad's not worth it. We're better off without him. It wasn't our fault. It wasn't. We didn't know.'

Frank dropped to his knees, forcing Peter to release him. He put his hands to his face while murmuring apologies and rocking back and forth.

Peter listened to Frank bleating with despair, then shrugged. Lincoln could only watch him in bemusement until with a sigh Chuck stepped forward.

'We killed Brad,' he said levelly. 'He was a good-for-nothing low-down snake and he had it coming a hundred times over. Everybody would have said so, except they won't now.'

'Why not?' Lincoln asked.

'Because while he was off on one of his no-good missions, he got sick. We didn't know that when we killed him, but we do now.'

Lincoln tipped back his hat as he considered the brothers. Now that their secret had been revealed Frank got to his feet. He and Chuck looked at each other with apparent relief. In Lincoln's experience guilty men spun ever more bizarre tales to prove their innocence, but these two were incriminating themselves further with everything they said.

'You could have said Brad died of the plague. With this much death around, you might have got away with it, so I'm inclined to believe you. Tell me what happened.'

'He returned to town all angry and shouting,' Chuck said, 'but he was weak and he said he was ill. We fought with him, thinking he was drunk, but he really was sick. He collapsed and he didn't get up again.'

Lincoln nodded. 'I'll believe you when I see the body.'

Chuck winced. 'That's the trouble. You can't. We dropped him down the deepest well. Then people started getting sick. . . .'

Chuck stood beside Frank and both men lowered their heads as they meekly awaited Lincoln's verdict on their fate. Peter joined Lincoln, his shoulders slumping as his anger faded away.

'I'll have to arrest you,' Lincoln said. He glanced around the muddy expanse. 'And someone will have to get his body out and properly buried. That'll help clean up the wells.'

Despite Lincoln's calm tone neither man answered, so he pushed them on. With Peter walking on one side and Lincoln on the other they escorted them to the fence and then back to town. But before the water wagon came back into view Lincoln heard a commotion rise up ahead.

This wasn't unexpected, as the appearance of water was sure to excite people who had been deprived of it. But when he reached the end of the road to his surprise it wasn't the ill south-side folk who were causing the trouble. Shelby and others from the north side had ventured out on to the main drag for the first time.

Lincoln drew Peter away to the corner of the end building to watch the developing situation. Weaver and Gail were standing before the water wagon. On the boardwalk opposite several men were edging along while eyeing the wagon.

Weaver bade Gail to back away, but she shook her head and stayed with him to face the approaching men. That sight decided it for Peter. He pushed past Lincoln and headed down the road. Lincoln didn't try to stop him; instead he escorted his prisoners down the road at a more leisurely pace.

'Get back, you men,' Peter shouted. 'This is our water.'

Her husband's voice made Gail swing round to face him. She mustered a brief smile, but Peter's arrival prompted Weaver to set off across the road. Despite Shelby's apparent aim of claiming the water, his approach made the men stop moving towards the wagon.

'And you men stay back,' Shelby shouted from the boardwalk. 'Keep your disease to yourself.'

Weaver spread his hands but he continued to advance.

'I'm pleased you've kept yourself safe, Shelby. What you did was sensible. I may not agree with—'

'Quit talking. The longer we stand out here, the more chance you'll kill us.'

Wisely Weaver stopped and kept quiet. When Peter joined Gail she held his arm with a gesture that appeared to ask if he'd calmed down. He returned a nod. Then he told her to stand behind the wagon while he joined Weaver.

Lincoln reckoned this was the right moment to make his presence known. He urged the brothers to move on quickly, his brief orders ensuring that Shelby glanced his way. Lincoln saw that several of Shelby's men had drawn guns, but they were holding them loosely while looking to Shelby for directions.

'Shelby,' Lincoln shouted, 'every time we meet you go down in my estimation.'

'We need water,' Shelby said. 'The beer's gone and we can't live on whiskey.'

'You can't, but you won't get water with guns.'

'If we can't have it, neither will you.'

Shelby gestured and several men swung their guns up, their targets the barrels on the back of the wagon. A few well-placed shots would hole the barrels and make them pour their life-giving water to the dirt.

Weaver ran back to the wagon and stood between the guns and the barrels while Peter drew his own gun. He aimed at Shelby.

'For every hole in a barrel,' he shouted, 'I'll put a hole in you.'

Lincoln kept his gun holstered as he advanced.

'No more threats,' he said. 'Nobody is shooting anyone or anything.'

For long moments the crowd all glanced at one another. Lincoln caught Peter's eye, judging that his hot-headed new helper would be the first to react, but when someone spoke it was Weaver.

'With rationing,' he said, 'there's enough water here for everyone. You people can have one barrel a day.'

Shelby licked his lips and moved forward for a hesitant pace. He eyed Lincoln, Peter, the barrels, then his men, weighing up the situation.

'Deal,' he said. 'As soon as you've backed away, we'll take one barrel only.'

Peter lowered his gun, closely followed by Shelby's men, making everyone sigh with relief as the tension in the situation dissipated. Lincoln waited until everyone had holstered their guns before he spoke up.

'You can do that, Shelby,' he said, 'provided you do something for me.'

CHAPTER 9

'It's Doc Weaver again,' Kyle said.

Nick nodded. As he drove the wagon on he peered ahead and tried to make out Weaver's demeanour. The chances of their plan succeeding relied on Weaver's at least paying up for yesterday's water, so that they could placate Ward. Nick had no doubt that if this time they returned short-changed he wouldn't be so accepting.

They were drawing the wagon to a halt fifty yards away from Weaver's wagon for this noon transfer when Weaver raised a bag. It appeared bulkier than yesterday's bag, making Nick relax.

'I have money,' Weaver called.

'Good,' Nick said. 'Does that mean you've found Marvin Sewell?'

'He's at large in town. We're trying to get him and your money.' Weaver patted the bag, then hurled it towards them. 'For now everyone has handed over every cent they had. I hope it's enough to keep you out of trouble.'

'I hope so too,' Nick said when it landed a few feet from the wagon. 'But whether you find the money or not, this must end now. We have to join forces to defy Ward.'

'We can't. Our efforts are devoted to keeping the disease under control.' Weaver shrugged. 'And besides, there's no need for you to get involved. Brad Ellison's dead.'

Nick nodded, finding no pleasure in this news.

'That doesn't change anything, and besides you have a lawman.'

Nick and Kyle then went on to outline their plan while manoeuvring barrels off the back of the wagon so that their behaviour would appear innocent to the nearest gunmen in the cordon. Tomorrow they hoped to hide as many men as possible on Weaver's wagon, transfer them, then launch a surprise ambush on Ward.

'Agreed,' Weaver said when they'd finished.

With that matter concluded, Kyle asked Weaver questions about what was happening in town, adding to the details he'd gathered yesterday. This time Weaver readily provided information and his lengthy responses suggested he'd prepared several of his answers beforehand.

Nick dallied for as long as possible in moving the last two barrels from the wagon while not risking raising suspicions. When the barrels were lined up on a slight rise, he lengthened out the exchange by gathering up the bag and counting out the money. It was less than Ward wanted, but Nick judged that it would be enough to satisfy him.

When Nick had finished Kyle still wanted more information, so he took the wagon away for a short distance. While Weaver loaded the barrels on to his wagon, Nick slowly counted the money for a second time and Kyle shouted out questions.

By the time Kyle had dried up the barrels were loaded up. They all wished each other well for tomorrow. Then Weaver moved the wagon off. Nick watched him leave, noting the steady drip of water from one of the barrels.

'A barrel's leaking again,' he said thoughtfully while still ruminating on the problems they'd face tomorrow.

'I hope enough water's left,' Kyle said. 'Perhaps if Peter hadn't hidden inside that barrel yesterday, it wouldn't be leaking so badly.'

'It's not his fault.' Nick watched the water flow increase when the wagon travelled over a stretch of rough ground. 'These are a fresh set of barrels. We're the only people who come close to the townsfolk.'

Kyle nodded, admitting his error, and so Nick moved the wagon on. They took a circuitous route back to the ridge that slipped between two groups of gunmen. This was the maximum distance from prying eyes they could manage, ensuring it wouldn't look out of place when they used the same route tomorrow.

Kyle was quiet, being as thoughtful as Nick was. They'd travelled for a quarter-mile when he sat up straight on the seat, then swirled round to look at the distant receding wagon. Nick followed his gaze.

'I was right,' Kyle murmured, his voice catching. 'That leaking barrel was the one Peter hid in yesterday.'

'A barrel's a barrel. Just because it leaks, it doesn't mean it's—'

'Be quiet!' Kyle snapped with a rare display of temper.

He closed his eyes then put a hand to his brow in a gesture of forcing himself to think harder. His expression was so serious that Nick drew back on the reins, halting the wagon.

'I don't see what's worrying you.'

Kyle didn't reply immediately. He rubbed his brow as if that would force him to think through his problem. Then he winced and looked up at Nick from under his hand.

'I'm right. Today's leaking barrel had a piece missing close to the rim, as did the barrel that Peter hid inside yesterday.'

Nick opened his mouth to object, but then his heart thudded as he pieced together the situation.

They delivered the barrels of water to Doctor Weaver. He distributed them. Then someone secretly brought the barrels back to Ward and they delivered them back to Weaver to complete the cycle. There was only one reason Nick could think of for Ward to do that.

'Ward's trying to profit from the Hope Wells disaster and the only problem on the horizon is that the townsfolk will one day fight off the disease.'

Kyle nodded. 'So Ward has to make sure they don't. The town wells are contaminated so the towns-folk want fresh water from the creek, but he's not sending them fresh water. He's got someone working for him in town who sends poisonous water out of town for him to deliver it back to them.'

'We're not helping to stop the disease,' Nick murmured aghast. 'We're spreading it.'

'And,' Kyle said with a pronounced gulp, 'I drank the water yesterday.'

Nick slapped his forehead. 'I made you do that to give us a distraction.'

The two men stared at each other until Kyle gave a wan smile.

'I don't blame you,' he murmured. 'We could be wrong, and even if we're not, I could get lucky.'

'You will,' Nick said with as much conviction as he could muster. 'You're young and healthy and you only had a sip.'

Kyle bit his lip as he looked towards the town. 'Not knowing is the worst, but I have to stop this situation getting any worse.'

'Agreed,' Nick said raising the reins. 'We need to warn them.'

Kyle slapped a hand on Nick's arm. 'You don't need to risk yourself; besides you can find out the truth from Ward.'

Nick considered, then nodded, accepting that dividing their forces was the best option.

'We'll still try to carry out the plan tomorrow,' he

said. 'But for now grab the reins, then hit me.'

'Hit you?'

'Not hard, but we need to make it look good for Ward.'

Kyle flashed a brief smile, then pushed Nick. It might have been because of his urgent need to get to town, but the blow was harder than Nick had expected and he didn't need to overplay his slide across the seat before he tumbled over the side.

He landed on all fours, where he stared at the ground for some moments, gathering his senses. By the time he looked up Kyle was moving the wagon off. Nick shook a fist at him, but then he had to dodge aside as Kyle hurled the saddle-bag at him.

Nick gave chase, but as he was in danger of catching the wagon, he limped along for several paces, then stumbled to his knees.

After that he contented himself with kicking dirt and throwing his hat to the ground while silently wishing Kyle well in his chase after the other wagon, which was now closing on town. He gathered up the saddle-bag and made his way to the ridge.

With every step he made his anger grew. He gripped his hands into tight fists and tried to keep his rage under control, but Ward's actions were just too callous for that to work. Profiting from the town's misfortune was bad enough, but perpetuating their woes was barbaric.

He reached the base of the ridge before anyone came to investigate. He was pleased that Ward was amongst the riders who approached. They were looking to town, then to Nick, clearly wondering what had happened. Nick stopped and waited for them to come to him.

'Get the money?' Ward asked when he'd drawn up before him.

Nick unhooked the saddle-bag from his shoulder and hurled it to the ground.

'Yeah,' he said, unable to keep the bitterness from his voice. 'Count it. I reckon you'll be pleased.'

Ward gave him an odd look, but he still dismounted and took the bag. The other riders edged forward to peer down at him as they awaited the verdict.

'I am pleased,' Ward said as he riffled through the bills, 'but stick to the plan and ask for more tomorrow. Hope Wells is clearly richer than they try to make out.'

'Hope Wells is dying.'

Ward looked up and moved towards him while waving a handful of money.

'It can do as long as they pay. But you did well.' He counted, then held out bills. 'Take your share. Now we all get to prosper.'

Nick knew he should take the money to continue giving the impression that he was working for Ward, but his anger was still making his heart race, so instead he fixed Ward with his gaze.

'Tell me one thing first,' he said. 'Where did you get the water?'

'Ah,' Ward said, withdrawing the hand. 'Is that why your young friend stole the wagon?'

'He drank the water. He was frightened.'

'Unfortunate for him, but fortunate for you.' Ward counted out more bills. 'You can have his share. He won't be coming back.'

Nick considered the bills, then moved over to gather them up, making Ward smile. That sight was too much for Nick.

He batted Ward's hand aside, sending the bills fluttering away. Then he put all his pent-up anger into a scything blow to Ward's cheek that sent him reeling.

'Blood money!' Nick roared standing over him.

Flat on his back, Ward fingered his face, wincing. He looked up at the surrounding riders and gave a small hand gesture.

As one the men dismounted and moved in.

CHAPTER 10

'What's to become of us?' Chuck Ellison asked.

Lincoln considered him and his brother through the bars. Weaver had confirmed that their actions had caused the plague outbreak, making their arrest a necessity, both to pay for the crimes and for their own protection from the wrath of the townsfolk.

'I don't know,' Lincoln said. 'But I doubt anyone will trust you with the town wells again.'

Chuck winced, then moved over to sit on his cot and cast worried looks at Frank.

The prisoners having been dealt with, Lincoln told Peter to keep watch. Peter nodded and sat behind the desk where he rested his feet on the top and glared across the room at his prisoners.

After a day spent with Peter, Lincoln judged him to be a man who was quick to anger and quick to act, but he was also competent, so he was relaxed about giving him duties.

He went outside, where he looked to the corner of the road that led to the north side. Shelby was standing on the edge of his self-assigned territory, looking out of town pensively as he awaited Weaver's return.

Lincoln caught his eye. Shelby gave a brief nod, acknowledging that he would honour his side of the deal provided Lincoln honoured his. So Lincoln paced out into the road and waited for the water wagon.

It took longer than Lincoln had expected; when he saw the wagon it was approaching town slowly, presumably to avoid spilling the expensive and precious water. Lincoln moved on to meet it.

'Four full barrels this time,' Weaver said as he drew the wagon up. 'And worth the cost if it helps everyone.'

Lincoln nodded. Yesterday morning's bleak outlook had improved today, presumably because of the fresh water. Nobody had died overnight and for the first time in a week the grave-diggers had stopped their activities.

'First we save this town, then I'll deal with Ward Dixon.'

'And that could be soon if you want. Nick and Kyle have a plan to take him on. They reckon we can smuggle people out on the water wagon and ambush Ward at the ridge.'

'Is that safe? I won't spread this plague, even to men like him.'

Weaver frowned. 'It probably isn't, but then again from the way Nick was talking, you wouldn't exactly be taking prisoners in the ambush.'

'I'll think about it. If I reckon the plan can work,

I'll. . . .' Lincoln trailed off on seeing that a second wagon was heading into town. 'Are you expecting that?'

'No,' Weaver said, narrowing his eyes. 'That's Kyle. Perhaps there's been a change of plan.'

'Perhaps, but I can't see why he's risking himself coming here.' Lincoln glanced away to see that a delegation from the north side of town was approaching. 'You talk to him. I'll get the water distributed and conclude my deal with Shelby.'

Weaver followed Lincoln's gaze to the corner of the road, where two men and Shelby were escorting Marvin Sewell towards them. While Weaver moved on to meet the wagon Lincoln looked out for signs of duplicity, but Marvin was scowling and struggling, forcing them to drag him along, suggesting that all was as it seemed.

'Water for Marvin,' Shelby said. 'That was the deal.'

'Bring him to me,' Lincoln said, 'while I get you today's barrel.'

Shelby signified that the men should move Marvin into the road, but only for a few paces.

Lincoln jumped on to the wagon and put his hands to the barrel, but the nearest one to the back was leaking and with the hardpan below he didn't want to risk breaking it. He waited for Weaver to return to help him, but when he looked up it was to see him hurrying out of the way of the still speeding wagon.

The wagon careered across the road so quickly it

almost rolled into the water wagon before with a desperate holler the young driver slowed the horses and veered them away.

'It's me, Kyle,' he shouted. 'Don't drink the water. Don't even touch it!'

The wagon carried on past Lincoln and came to a halt forty yards on. Lincoln looked at Shelby, who glared at the barrels with a mixture of horror and confusion. Lincoln jumped down and with Weaver he headed on to Kyle.

'We've paid for the water!' Weaver said. 'We're not paying any—'

'It's not about the money,' Kyle said. He climbed down to face them and wrung his hands, worry making his eyes wide. 'It's the water. It's contaminated.'

'Only the water that comes from our wells is dangerous. From the creek it'll be fine.'

Kyle rubbed his brow while looking at the group by the corner. He gulped before he replied.

'That's the problem. The barrels were filled here, taken out of town secretly, then brought back for you to buy them all over again.'

'Why would anyone. . . ?' Weaver trailed off. He looked at Lincoln with the same forlorn look that Kyle was sporting.

'To make sure we never defeat the plague,' Lincoln murmured.

'Nobody would be so desperate to make money that they'd kill a whole town, surely?'

Kyle gave a sorry shake of the head that said the

men he'd dealt with would.

'Then they've made a big mistake,' Lincoln said. 'I'll round up every last one of them. When I've finished with them they'll reckon getting the plague would be less painful.'

Lincoln considered his forces. Aside from Peter in the law office he didn't have many options for gathering fit men for such an assault. That made him look to Shelby and his group, and with a wince he saw that these men were muttering to themselves, their tones angry.

When the debate ended Shelby pointed an accusing finger at him.

'You've killed us!' he roared.

'I haven't,' Lincoln said. 'The man who swapped the barrels put you in danger, this Ward—'

'I don't care about him. I just know I kept the plague at bay for a week and then the first time I got help, you gave me poisoned water.'

Lincoln couldn't blame Shelby for being angry, so he thought carefully about his next comment, hoping that once Shelby had calmed down he could deflect him into positive action.

'We don't know that for sure,' he said, walking towards him and using a soft tone. 'The water might not be from the wells, after all, and even if it is, it isn't certain that anyone who's drunk it will be affected. We need to stay calm until we know the full facts.'

He looked to Weaver for support. He nodded, but Lincoln's reasonable statement had aggrieved Shelby even more. He glared at Lincoln, then at the barrels and then at the law office.

'Agreed,' he muttered with steady menace. 'We do need to find out the truth. And I'll do just that.'

Shelby took two determined paces, but then he thought better of getting too close to Lincoln and with a beckoning gesture he urged his men to join him in taking a circuitous route across the road.

'What are you doing?' Lincoln said, moving to block him.

'You're the lawman. You should have figured out already that the Ellison brothers have been sneaking poisoned water out of town.'

Shelby gave Lincoln a long look then turned to the law office forcing Lincoln to raise a hand.

'No further,' he said. 'You had the right idea about keeping your distance. I'll find out what the Ellison brothers have been doing.'

Shelby started to object but Lincoln didn't continue the argument and so risk goading Shelby into taking the matter into his own hands. He returned to the wagon and instructed Weaver to guard the water. Then he headed to the law office.

Inside, Peter winced on seeing Lincoln's determined posture, then he gathered up the keys to the cells without being asked. But Lincoln shook his head and paced up to the bars to face his prisoners.

Chuck was the first to look up.

'You ready to let us go?' he asked, his wide smile suggesting he was attempting a joke.

'You'd better hope I don't. You'll be dead the

moment you step through the door.'

Chuck exchanged a glance with Frank. Both brothers shrugged.

'We've been facing that for a week.'

Lincoln paced back and forth in front of the cell door, stretching out the moment before he revealed the latest development, hoping it'd worry them into offering the truth before he had to drag it out of them. With a stomp of his feet he came to a halt, then swung round to face the bars. He grabbed one in each hand and considered the prisoners.

'It's hardly surprising when you've been distributing water despite Brad's body being down the well.'

Chuck narrowed his eyes as he considered Lincoln, then pointed at him.

'If someone's been taking the water, that's not our fault.'

Lincoln had spent too much time with men such as Chuck and Frank to believe their protestations of innocence, but in this case the fate of a town lay in the balance and he had to uncover the truth. He studied both men carefully as he spoke.

'So you've seen someone take it?'

While Frank grumbled to himself Chuck waved a dismissive hand at him, then returned to his cot where he contemplated him with a surly eye.

'I'm not talking and letting you twist my words.'

'Ward Dixon has been selling your well water back to the town.' Lincoln pointed to the coffee pot sitting on the stove. 'That's the water we've all been drinking. I want to know how he got it.'

Chuck paled. 'We wouldn't be so stupid as to poison ourselves.'

Lincoln judged that the frightened looks the brothers were shooting at each other were genuine, and he had to admit Chuck's explanation was a good one. No matter how misguided their behaviour, they wouldn't gamble with their own lives for profit, and yesterday they'd not had much time to effect a transfer before he'd arrested them.

He slapped the bars in frustration, then turned to Peter, who was gulping while cringing away from an empty coffee mug on the desk.

'Is that what the commotion was about outside?' he asked.

'Yeah. Nobody's happy about it.'

'I need to check on Gail.'

Lincoln gave a brief nod. Peter wasted no time in hurrying to the door, but when he reached it he came to a sudden halt. He stood for a moment, then gestured for Lincoln to approach.

When Lincoln looked outside he had to join Peter in wincing. Shelby had gathered the denizens of the north side about him. They were standing in a line on the edge of their territory, eyeing the law office as they awaited his verdict. Amongst the men stood Marvin Sewell, now free and relaxed.

'Chuck and Frank sounded convincing to me,' Lincoln said, 'but I don't reckon their tale will convince Shelby.'

'And I doubt we can stop him if he comes,' Peter said.

Lincoln nodded. 'In that case get your wife and Weaver here. I reckon a new siege is about to begin.'

CHAPTER 11

The waiting game had begun.

Peter brought Kyle to the office. Then he went to the south side and found Gail and Doctor Weaver. They joined Lincoln in the law office, but as the sun set and Shelby didn't make his move, the tension between Weaver and Peter made everyone nervous.

Weaver sat close to the cells watching the prisoners, perhaps trying to work out whether they had poisoned the water deliberately, or perhaps just to avoid looking at Peter. For his part Peter never moved far from his wife, and he continually shot Weaver surly glares that suggested he was awaiting an opportunity to confront him.

The acrimony encouraged Kyle to stay close to Lincoln who, when he wasn't looking outside, studied his new companions. When Peter looked elsewhere Weaver looked at Gail, but whether his intentions were lustful or friendly, Lincoln couldn't tell. The fact that Gail rarely looked at him suggested that at best his desires were unrequited.

Either way, Lincoln harboured no ill-feeling towards Weaver. The man had done more than anyone could have expected to keep the town alive and he couldn't blame him if he'd tried to reach out to someone for comfort.

'I can't just sit here all evening too,' Weaver said, speaking for the first time in hours.

'We need to do what Lincoln says,' Peter said immediately, proving that he had been waiting for an opportunity to argue with him.

'You do,' Weaver said wearily as he stood up, 'but I need to check on how everyone is faring before I can settle down for the night.'

Gail moved to rise too, but Peter shook his head.

'You're not going with him,' he snapped, then he lowered his tone to a more reasonable one. 'It's too dangerous.'

'I agree,' Weaver said as Gail started to object. 'And besides, she should stay to monitor how you're all doing. You did, after all, drink the water too.'

This reminder made Lincoln's guts churn, as they did every time he thought about the possibility. He'd made the mistake of asking Weaver what the first symptoms were, so every time he thought about the danger he couldn't help but think that he was getting hotter and weaker.

'As did you,' Lincoln said.

'I'll monitor myself,' Weaver said.

'And if your patrol goes well?'

'When we holed up in here nobody new had got ill today. If that continues there's a good chance we got

94

lucky and the water isn't as tainted as we feared.'

Lincoln nodded. 'If that proves to be the case, I'll see whether Shelby will let you check on him and his people. Good news might persuade him to calm down.'

'It might,' Weaver said, 'but then again bad news might bring an attack forward.'

'If it's bad news, then there's no hope for any of us.'

Weaver frowned then headed to the door, but he stopped in the doorway.

'I'll be gone for an hour,' he said, then offered everyone a hopeful smile.

Lincoln nodded and Weaver slipped off into the gathering darkness leaving the others to keep lookout and to revert to silence.

The next hour dragged. As darkness settled, several times Lincoln saw movement outside and he slipped through the door. But every time it turned out to be people from the south side venturing out on to the main drag for the first time in a while.

These sightings gave Lincoln hope that Weaver had been right. Perhaps the plague had done its worst and the contaminated water hadn't brought about a relapse.

On the north side he saw no movement, but he didn't doubt that eyes were on the law office as Shelby awaited his moment to attack. But when he caught the first inkling of trouble it came from an unexpected direction.

From the east and along the route he had taken to

come into town the open wagon that Weaver had been using to ferry in the water appeared. Weaver wasn't on it, but two men he'd seen on the north side were up front with others sitting in the back.

The wagon drew up on the opposite side of the road. Shelby jumped down from the back to stand in a pool of moonlight, facing the law office. He was scowling.

'Peter, come with me,' Lincoln said with quiet authority. 'Gail, find Doctor Weaver. Kyle, cover us.'

Fortunately, Peter didn't object to this order; after urging Gail to hurry he slipped outside with Lincoln. He watched her until she disappeared around the corner heading to the south side, then he stood beside Lincoln.

'We've come for the Ellison brothers,' Shelby said, his announcement being backed up by two men jumping down from the wagon to flank him.

'They're under arrest,' Lincoln said. 'They're going nowhere.'

Shelby gestured back at the men who had stayed on the wagon.

'We don't agree. We've just buried Ford Varley. He was the first from our side of town to die after you poisoned us. I doubt he'll be the last. We aim to fight back before we have to bury anyone else.'

Lincoln considered, searching for the right thing to say, but Peter shook his head, then spoke up first.

'Ford Varley was old when this town was founded and he spent every day shuffling from one saloon to the next. Him dying doesn't mean the plague's come to you.'

'It takes the old and the weak first, but when it's taken hold it's no respecter of age or strength.'

Lincoln couldn't retort with any conviction, so he looked down the road towards the south side. Gail was returning, but there was no sign yet of Weaver.

'Where is Doctor Weaver?' he said to Peter. 'He's the only one who can stop this confrontation.'

Peter gave a worried nod as Shelby and his men moved towards them with determined paces and with their guns drawn. Then Peter followed Lincoln's gaze to see Gail. He gestured at her to stay away, but she ignored him and broke into a run.

Peter continued to shoo her away until she reached him. Then, with a shake of the head, he grabbed her arm and manoeuvred her into the law office. Lincoln checked that she was out of danger, receiving a nod from Peter in the doorway. Then he faced the advancing Shelby.

Lincoln knew that the moment he joined Peter inside a siege would develop. Then, trapped in the law office, he would no longer be in control of the situation. So he stood his ground.

'Hand them over,' Shelby said, stopping ten yards from Lincoln, this being the usual distance he kept between him and anyone from outside his territory.

'The only handing over to be done is you giving me Marvin Sewell.'

'Marvin!' Shelby spluttered. 'The deal was him for water, not him for death.'

'You don't know that yet. Wait until Doctor Weaver

returns before you do anything foolish. He was treating the south side successfully and there's been no deaths in over a day.'

'Except for Ford Varley.'

'Perhaps, but Weaver is the only one who can help you, so you have to decide whether revenge is more important than living.'

Shelby firmed his jaw, making Lincoln flex his hand in preparation for going for his gun, but then Shelby nodded briefly.

'You have one hour to bring him here. If he can convince me we'll live, I'll back off. If not, I'll take the Ellison brothers and anyone who stands in my way.'

Without further comment Shelby gathered his men around him. A brief debate ensued with much nodding and a few glares at the law office before everyone trooped off down the road. Lincoln watched them to ensure that they all left, then, aware of the increasing urgency of the situation, he abandoned the law office.

He sent Gail and Peter to search the south side, this time more thoroughly, while he covered the rest of town that he was able to visit. He doubted that Weaver would have sneaked into the north side.

With Kyle he searched along the main drag where he could keep an eye on the office.

They found no sign of Weaver in any of the buildings on the main drag. When they returned to the road that led to the south side, Lincoln saw Gail and Peter scurrying from building to building with desperate haste.

When they saw him they gave exaggerated shrugs and headshakes that Lincoln took to mean that not only could they not find Weaver, nobody else knew where he was either.

They'd used up most of their allotted time when Lincoln decided it was unlikely that Weaver was still in town. So he and Kyle headed off to search the surrounding area. They'd walked only a few yards past the endmost building when Kyle drew his attention and pointed. The gate to the wells was swinging open.

Lincoln frowned. He had started searching at the other end of the road, having dismissed the Ellisons' property as being somewhere Weaver was likely to have visited. He put aside his irritation and with Kyle he hurried on to their building, but it was deserted, and Weaver did not respond when they called for him.

It was only when they turned to go that Lincoln noticed that something had changed since yesterday, but in the gloom he wasn't sure what. He told Kyle to throw the doors wide to let in as much light as possible while he summoned up an image of the layout. Then he looked around and this time he saw the space that hadn't been there yesterday.

A wagon had been standing by the wall and he reckoned that now there weren't as many barrels as there had been previously.

'Weaver, you're a wise, but foolish man,' Lincoln said. Then, when Kyle looked at him quizzically, he explained. 'After you brought in the contaminated water, Weaver must have realized that the only way this town will recover is by drinking clean water again. He's tried to sneak out to the creek to get it for himself.'

When they came out of the building Kyle looked into the darkness towards the ridge and the creek beyond.

'He probably didn't want to endanger anyone else with his reckless scheme,' he said. 'But the cordon is patrolled by ruthless men and they're situated at regular intervals. Even in the dark he'll need plenty of luck to get through and back.'

'Then I wish him that luck. Clean water probably is the only thing that'll head off this situation.'

With the mystery seemingly resolved Lincoln headed back to town, where he called for Peter and Gail to join them. For the first time Peter nodded with approval at Weaver's actions while Gail cast worried glances out of town.

In a pensive mood they walked down the main drag to the law office. Lincoln hurried on ahead. He confirmed that the Ellisons were still in their cell, but when he looked out through the door to beckon the others in, they gestured for him to join them instead.

Lincoln soon saw what the problem was. Shelby was approaching.

'Your hour's up,' Shelby called. 'Bring Weaver here now or bring me the Ellisons.'

CHAPTER 12

'Thirsty?' Ward asked.

'Sure,' Nick said, figuring that remaining on pleasant terms with his captor would give him his best chance of surviving.

Since Nick had punched Ward several hours ago no retaliation had come. Ward's men had merely escorted him to the ridge, then bound his hands.

Now, with the sun lowering, Ward was showing an interest in him. Nick presumed the delay had let him devise a suitable punishment.

Ward gestured to someone out of Nick's view. Creaking sounded and a barrel came into view, being rolled at an angle and with water sloshing over the sides. It was the same kind as they'd taken to Hope Wells earlier.

While keeping Nick in view Ward went over to the barrel and held out a hand. A ladle was slapped into his palm and he used the handle to prise off the lid. He dipped the ladle in the water and then, taking care to avoid spilling a drop, he brought it over to Nick.

Ward's slow walk gave Nick time to think, but he couldn't decide what he should do. The water could be polluted, or then again it might not be.

Nick stood to meet him and set his feet wide apart in a confident manner. His hands were tied behind his back securely but it would be easy to avoid the water if he chose to.

Ward brought the ladle up while watching for his reaction. Only when Nick could look down at the still water did he jerk his head away.

Ward lowered his hand and poured the water on the ground. Nick turned back to see that he was smiling.

'You've lost faith in water,' Ward said. He threw the ladle aside then wiped his hands on his jacket as if to remove all traces of the tainted water. 'We can't have that.'

Ward clicked his fingers and two men moved in purposefully.

Nick stood his ground, not wanting to give Ward the satisfaction of seeing him struggle, but when the men grabbed his arms and moved him on towards the barrel he couldn't help but dig in his heels.

The men shoved and he stumbled on for several paces before he halted himself. Then, with a shrug of his shoulders he threw off one of the men. This only encouraged another man to come up from behind and help the first man move him on towards the barrel.

They had to shove him with his boots digging twin furrows in the ground but despite his best efforts he bellied up against the barrel.

'Drink it dry,' one man said, 'and we let you go.'

Then, with two men holding an arm apiece, the third man slapped a hand on the back of his head and pushed, aiming to dunk his head in the barrel.

Nick kept himself upright for several seconds, but then one of the men slapped him in the stomach, bending him double and making him gasp.

With his mouth wide open, his head was forced down towards the water. At the last moment he gasped in a breath of air and closed his mouth. Then his head slipped below the surface.

He resisted the urge to struggle as he conserved his strength. He doubted they were aiming to drown him, but that hope receded as his count reached fifty and buzzing sounded in his ears along with the rising urge to struggle.

Through his ordeal he kept his mouth clamped tightly shut until he was yanked up.

He dragged in a long breath, then he was thrust under the water again. Once more he managed to keep his composure and came up gasping without taking in water, but on the third time they varied the method.

His head was thrust forward, but he wasn't shoved under water; he was left with his belly pressed against the rim and the water rippling inches from his nose.

Nick stared at the water with his breath held, but when he'd been held for almost a minute he drew in

103

a reedy wheeze of air through pursed lips. That was the moment when he was shoved in.

This time, within seconds of going under the water, his lungs demanded air and, which made it worse, the men holding him jostled him, forcing him to fight back. Almost without his realizing what had happened his mouth opened and cold water seeped in.

He struggled and raised his head from the water to spit it out, but immediately he was shoved back in and more water slipped in. He gave up any pretence of acting calmly; he fought and kicked but the three men had firm grips and they dictated when he went under and when he came up.

He was unable to fight back; water filled his mouth and when he next came up he couldn't help but swallow some of it before he gathered his breath. Now that he had taken his first drink some of the fight went out of him and they easily made him drink more.

Again and again they dunked him down and every time more of the cold water seeped down to his belly. By the time they relented and dragged him upright to face Ward, his stomach was bloated and the only comfort he had was that he reckoned he'd vomit some of the water back up soon.

'Had your fill?' Ward asked.

'Yeah, so you can take my place,' Nick said, 'and enjoy what the townsfolk are getting.'

'You don't sound as if you regret what you did.'

Ward raised his eyebrows with an invitation for

Nick to relent, but the anger that had made Nick hit Ward was hammering at his mind and defeating any thoughts of calming down.

'Do you?' he snapped.

Ward sneered, then looked to the men holding him. He gave a brief flipping gesture.

Nick didn't know what it meant, but he soon found out. He was bent double again. Then two men grabbed his legs and raised them.

They held him off the ground with his head aimed downwards and moved to the barrel. His head hit the water, closely followed by his shoulders and body. He slid down through the cold water until with a thud his head fetched up against the bottom. His legs were still outside the barrel and he kicked out but that only helped to mash his face against the bottom.

He managed one more kick, then he was breathing and coughing water. He suffered an endless moment of gut-wrenching fear, but then peace and darkness descended.

The sound of trickling water came to him. This felt odd and to his surprise he realized that he was also breathing shallowly. He glanced around and found that his face was no longer pressed to the base of the barrel, but he was still inches from the bottom.

He realized what must have happened. He had struggled strongly enough to topple the barrel and let the water pour out. Now he was lying on the ground with his head in the emptied barrel.

He didn't struggle when they dragged him out and stood him upright to face Ward. He couldn't; he was

105

bedraggled and half-drowned.

'Had your fill now?' Ward asked.

'Yeah,' Nick murmured, now shivering and unable to summon the strength even to appear defiant.

'And so now we wait for you to die.' Ward signified that the men should make him sit. 'I've heard the plague takes hold quickly and its victims die in agony. Perhaps watching you die slowly will persuade me I'm doing the wrong thing.'

'For your sake I hope it does,' Nick said. 'This plague is dangerous and you and your men got wet when the water slopped everywhere.'

Ward yawned, then moved off to talk with his men. Despite his deliberate action, which could have been to mask his concern, Nick didn't get the impression that he was worried.

Nick couldn't say the same about himself. For the next few hours his concern increased, making his head throb and his guts clench with fear. After drinking so much water he was sick several times. He hoped that that would be enough to stave off the effects of the poisoned water, but other than waiting he could do nothing.

Time passed slowly. He tried not to dwell on whether his thudding heart and coldness were signs of a developing fever. As the sun set the group became animated, at least providing him with a distraction, with two groups returning from their patrols and others leaving to make their own night patrols.

They all had reports that interested Ward. Nick

tried to overhear the details, but they talked too quietly for him to hear.

It was some hours since Kyle had passed on the news of the new threat to Hope Wells and Nick expected that the townsfolk would have reacted by now, but so far he'd heard nothing. He still hoped they'd act as he was unlikely to be in a position to help them mount the raid they'd planned to make on the following day.

After talking with his men Ward returned and stood over him.

'You look worried,' he said. 'Perhaps I should fetch a doctor.'

'Send me to Hope Wells instead,' Nick said. 'There's a doctor there.'

'Is there?' Ward looked into the darkness. A wagon was trundling closer and several men were moving into position to welcome its arrival. 'I don't reckon you're going anywhere.'

'I won't spread the plague, but I sure don't want to die here with you watching me.'

Ward drew the attention of the men who weren't waiting for the wagon and ordered them to watch over Nick. Then he went over to the upturned barrel. He righted it, then found the ladle and filled it with the dregs of water. Still smiling he came over to Nick and held out the ladle.

'Drink?' he asked, smirking.

'I'm not thirsty,' Nick said. 'You drink it.'

Nick had meant his comment to be sarcastic, but Ward nodded. With his gaze set on him he brought

107

the ladle to his lips and upended it.

Nick stared at him in amazement as he wiped his mouth with the back of his hand. Then Ward tossed the ladle to another one of his men, who wasted no time in fetching water for himself.

'Is there a problem?' Ward said.

For long moments Nick stared at Ward and it was only when he laughed that Nick looked skyward and blew out his cheeks with relief.

'The water's not poisoned,' he murmured.

'It sure isn't,' Ward said, licking his lips. 'This water came from the creek. So have you learnt a valuable lesson?'

'Yeah,' Nick murmured. He nodded, acknowledging he had been fooled, after which he willed his racing heart to slow while he enjoyed the fact that he wouldn't be dying in agony some time soon.

Ward even removed his bonds, giving him hope that he might be allowed to continue working for him. While he awaited news on his fate, he looked at the approaching wagon, which was now close enough for him to see that several barrels were on the back.

'The question now,' Ward said, 'is whether you need another lesson. This wagon has our next delivery of water from Hope Wells, and this water will kill you.'

Nick said nothing as the wagon drew to a halt. The driver had lowered his head, masking his identity, but although Nick had only met one person from Hope Wells he was sure he'd seen him before.

When Ward moved over to talk with him, the man looked up, letting Nick see his features. Nick winced.

It was Doctor Weaver.

CHAPTER 13

'Howdy, Nick,' Doctor Weaver said, his tone light. 'You look shocked.'

'I am,' Nick said guardedly, still hoping that he was wrong about the situation and that Weaver was engaged in legitimate business.

Those hopes fled when Ward beckoned everyone to unload the barrels with care. His men treated the barrels differently from the barrel in which they'd dunked him. They only touched the dry sections of wood and they kept their faces averted.

Whether or not that would help, Nick didn't know and everyone's worried expressions showed they were unsure too. Nick stood back and Weaver at least had sufficient shame in his actions not to catch his eye until the men had completed the work.

'Do you want an explanation?' Weaver said.

'I doubt I'd understand,' Nick said, unable to stop irritation from straining his voice. 'Never harm nobody is what you doctors are supposed to do, isn't it?'

110

Weaver considered him, his eyes sad. He gestured to Ward.

Two men moved in and grabbed Nick's arms. Nick resisted the urge to struggle.

'That's not the creed, but you got its essence.' Weaver walked back to the wagon and returned with a small black bag. 'It's not my fault people are so stupid that they'll drink polluted water when it's pronounced safe by a man with a black bag.'

'You can't blame this on others,' Nick spluttered. He tried to advance on Weaver, but the men holding him dragged him back.

'But I can. And especially you for bringing Peter Campbell to town.'

Nick stared at Weaver, lost for words. Peter had seemed a decent man, if hot-headed, but he couldn't see why his unselfish efforts to be with his wife should have annoyed the doctor. Then he saw the glazed look in Weaver's eyes and he nodded.

'Peter said she'd come to town to help you nurse the sick, but he was worried about something else. And he had good cause, didn't he?'

'In time he would have. Gail and I were working closely, like we used to, but now that he's arrived it's all changed.'

Nick opened his mouth to say more, but then thought better of it. He had nothing to say to a man who had prolonged the suffering of an entire town just so he could spend more time with his nurse.

'If you've finished talking,' Ward said, coming over to them, 'I have a problem. I don't want another body with a bullet in it that I might have to explain away. I'd hoped your black bag would have another option.'

Weaver nodded, then withdrew a vial from his bag. He held it up to the limited light, ensuring that Nick saw it. Then, with a smirk on his face he advanced on Nick, who pressed himself back against the men holding him.

They tightened their grips, but with the uncertain fate that the vial promised fuelling him on, Nick bucked and shook them.

He tore an arm free from one man's grasp, and then launched a scything punch at the second man, which sent him tumbling to his knees, but he kept his firm grip of Nick's arm and dragged him down with him. Then another man joined in the fray and leapt on Nick's back.

On his knees Nick looked into the darkness, judging that if they weren't going to shoot him he stood a chance of running and holing up somewhere on the ridge.

He rolled his shoulders, then drove himself up from the ground, sending the man on his back flying. Then he used his momentum to pull his arm free. He turned to the freedom that beckoned him from the blackness ahead.

An arm was wrapped around his neck and a wad of damp cloth was slapped over his mouth and nose. Acrid fumes filled his nostrils, bringing with them a closer and more troubling form of blackness.

He breathed out, forcing away the lethal substance

112

that Weaver was trying to use on him, then he elbowed the doctor in the stomach. The blow had no force behind it. His limbs barely moved.

He stumbled forward on to his knees and then fetched up on his chest. All the time Weaver pressed the cloth over his face.

Fumes filled his lungs. Blackness embraced him.

'Weaver is out of town,' Lincoln said. 'I reckon he's helping this town live by bringing us fresh water.'

'If he's left town,' Shelby said, 'he'll have been killed. From what I've heard, Ward Dixon is ruthless.'

Lincoln firmed his jaw to avoid showing he thought this a likely outcome.

'We owe it to him and the risk he's taking to wait.'

'I can wait.' Shelby moved forward for a pace. 'But the Ellisons will be my guests.'

'You've threatened me once too often, Shelby.'

From the corner of his eye Lincoln saw that a dozen men had congregated at the corner of the road. He took the fact they hadn't advanced as a sign of their uncertainty about taking on the law. If that were the case, he needed to defeat only the lead man. With determined paces he advanced on Shelby.

His opponent stood his ground, but when he saw that Lincoln wasn't going to stop he backed away for a pace and then another. Lincoln maintained his movement, advancing faster than Shelby could back away and getting within the ten-yard safety range Shelby had maintained so far.

This proved to be too much for Shelby and he

sidestepped, then moved to run away, but in his haste he slipped and went to his knees.

Quickly he swivelled round to lie on his back where he raised a hand.

'No further,' he demanded, his eyes fearful.

Lincoln took another pace, then stomped to a halt. He noted that other men were moving in the shadows beneath the covered boardwalk opposite, but Shelby's behaviour also made him realize that he had one advantage. He looked over his shoulder at Peter and Kyle, then bade them approach.

The two men looked at each, clearly questioning whether they'd understood his instruction correctly, as Lincoln had told them to guard the law office. But on seeing Shelby shuffling away on his back they nodded.

They both made for the corner of the road, so cutting off the men who had been taking up attacking positions.

'I know you want to avoid shooting up a marshal,' Lincoln said, 'but I also know you want to avoid me.'

Lincoln took another slow pace, making Shelby stop moving backwards along the ground and seek to gain his feet. Lincoln speeded up. He took three long paces, then slapped a hand on the back of Shelby's jacket and helped him up.

Shelby tried to shake him off, but Lincoln gathered a better grip. Then he swung him round and grabbed his shoulders with both hands, forcing Shelby to look him in the eye. He took a deep breath and exhaled. Shelby cringed away and struggled to escape, making Lincoln laugh.

'Let me go,' Shelby muttered.

'Never. If anyone shoots me now I'll bleed all over you, and that sure won't be healthy for you.'

Shelby cast a forlorn look at the men in the shadows, but these men had problems of their own to deal with as they sought to avoid the advancing Kyle and Peter. Shelby attempted again to shake Lincoln off, but when that failed his shoulders slumped.

'What do you want of me, Marshal?' he asked, not meeting his eye, as if by avoiding looking at him he could keep the plague at bay.

'I want this town to return to the way it used to be run with the law in charge. You can accept that, or not.' Lincoln drew Shelby up close. 'I hope for your sake that you accept it.'

Slowly Shelby raised his head. Unexpectedly he was smiling. His gaze darted past Lincoln's shoulder before he looked at him.

'I refuse your offer,' he said with calm assurance. 'I hope for your sake that you accept mine.'

Lincoln wasn't easily distracted; so he resisted the urge to look over his shoulder, but he noticed that Kyle had stopped and that he was looking at the law office. Shelby snorted a laugh under his breath and in irritation Lincoln pushed him away.

He swirled round and set off. Gail was no longer standing outside and Peter was running. Lincoln ran faster than Peter did and he pounded up on to the boardwalk first. He veered to the side of the door and pressed his back to the wall.

Peter followed him, but with the fate of his wife uncertain he charged on, kicking the door with the sole of his boot then darting in through the opening door.

Lincoln had no choice but to follow him. He went in ducking and moving to the right. He stopped after two paces.

Peter was already raising his hands and looking to Lincoln to do the same. A glance around the law office revealed the reason why.

While Shelby had been exaggerating his terror at Lincoln's getting too close to him, Marvin had sneaked inside. Now he was standing by the cells with a gun pressed to Gail's side.

'And now,' he said, 'Shelby gets the Ellison brothers while you get to be my prisoner.'

CHAPTER 14

'So you'll be visiting Hope Wells at last, Nick,' Weaver said. His voice seemed to come from a great distance. 'But you'll have to stay quiet and still.'

Weaver chuckled, making Nick try to turn to him, but he didn't move. He noted, in a distracted way, that he couldn't see anything either, but he assumed that that meant it was still night. With his thoughts coming slowly, as if every memory was a great weight that he had to pick up and drag across his mind, he thought back to the last events that he could recall.

Ward had told Weaver to kill him, but the doctor had drugged him instead. Then he'd forced him to drink water that this time he knew was polluted.

As he'd been struggling to remain conscious for even a few seconds at a time he'd been unable to stop them pouring a considerable amount of water down his throat. Then he had passed out.

Worryingly, that troubling memory didn't perturb him. His senses were too befuddled.

'I'll take your failure to speak as a yes,' Weaver said

with amusement in his tone. A hand slapped down on Nick's shoulder and shook him, the impact feeling distant, as if it were happening to someone else. 'But I know you're awake.'

'What have you done to me?' Nick said, or at least he formed the thoughts and tried to speak, but Weaver didn't respond so he assumed he hadn't spoken aloud.

Despite this failure he noticed dim lights dancing around. He watched them, trying to discern what they were. Their movement was rhythmic and after a while he noticed that he was moving with the same rhythm.

As he went on, using his usual slow thought processes, understanding came. He was on the seat of the water wagon, sitting beside Weaver. They were closing on Hope Wells.

'You should find what's about to happen interesting,' Weaver said. 'Finding a way to let you die from the plague while at the same time completing my plans have come together in a single neat solution.'

'Go to hell,' Nick muttered, but again Weaver didn't react.

Ahead the lights brightened until Nick confirmed they had reached the main route into Hope Wells. His view tipped to the side and it was several seconds before his sluggish senses told him that Weaver had drawn the wagon to a halt and that the lurch had made him topple over on to his side.

Weaver snorted, presumably in appreciation of his new position. Then he waited to be noticed.

Nick couldn't focus his eyes properly; he was merely aware of the figures who emerged from down the road and approached the wagon.

'No further!' Weaver called, halting them. He jumped down from the wagon. 'I have a sick man here.'

'You don't give the orders now,' a man said. Nick didn't recognize his voice. 'I've taken over. You can help me only if you can convince me you'll follow my new regime.'

'You haven't taken over,' Weaver said, the steel in his voice that had surprised Nick earlier making the man back away for a pace. 'I'm the only one who can save you. So the question is: do you fit into my new regime.'

Doctor Weaver was back.

Shelby and his men were keeping Lincoln under close guard on the boardwalk outside the law office, but he was watching developments with interest, hoping for a distraction. The Ellison brothers were still in the law office, Weaver's arrival coming in time to save them from being taken away, but Lincoln had no doubt this was only a delay. With several men staying inside to taunt them about their fate, Lincoln reckoned they'd be lucky to see sunup.

When he glanced at Peter, he nodded, acknowledging he was looking for an opening too, but Kyle was staring at the comatose man on Weaver's wagon with concern. When Lincoln followed his gaze he saw that it was Nick Mitchell from White Ridge.

119

'We're taking control of our own lives, Weaver,' Shelby said.

'Then you'll die,' Weaver said. 'Your only hope is to trust me.'

'You brought back the poisoned water and that means we can never completely trust you again.'

'I didn't know that at the time.' Weaver gestured to the wagon where four barrels were lined up. 'But I got through Ward's cordon. I've brought back untainted water from the creek.'

Unbidden, Shelby's men moved towards the wagon. After a few moments Shelby nodded with approval.

'You did well. That's—'

'Stay away!' Weaver ordered, taking a backward step and spreading his arms before the wagon. 'This water will give life, but I'd sooner pour it away than let it be misused.'

'We're thirsty. We need it, and we'll take it.'

'That attitude will kill us all.' Weaver pointed at Nick. 'This man caught the plague and he's not from Hope Wells. He's the friend of one of the water carriers.'

Weaver looked at Kyle, who nodded, and the news made Shelby call out for everyone to back away from the wagon.

'Why are you bringing sick people here?' he asked.

'Because this town is sick and I can't let that sickness spread. We do what's best for everyone and that'll give us our best chance of surviving.' Weaver lowered his tone to his usual sympathetic one. 'I don't want to rule this town, but I have to. So follow me, or die.'

Shelby and Weaver glared at each other until Shelby, despite his earlier truculence, gave a brief nod.

'Tell me your plan. If I agree with it, you can advise me.'

For long moments silence reigned and Lincoln reckoned Weaver would defy Shelby, but he gave a slight smile.

'We combine our two methods and keep the well people apart from the sick, no matter who they are and no matter which side of town they're from.' Weaver smiled grimly. 'It's a heartless way, which could lead to your death or even mine, but it'll ensure everyone else's survival.'

Shelby gulped, then glanced around his gathered men who, after this confirmation that nobody was immune, were looking at him with doubt for the first time.

'We'll do that,' he said. 'I'll always act in the best interests of the town.'

'Then I'll begin by checking our health.' Weaver considered the gathered people until his gaze fell on Lincoln. 'Bring me the lawman first.'

'Why him?'

'Because he was handing out the water yesterday.' Weaver folded his arms and gave an ingratiating smile. 'But of course only if that's acceptable to you.'

Shelby snorted his breath, but then he beckoned for Lincoln to be brought forward. Lincoln expected that Weaver would catch his eye or in some way convey what was his real plan to defeat Shelby, but instead he adopted his efficient professional manner.

Weaver looked him over, felt his forehead, his pulse, turned him to look into his eyes using the best light coming from an oil lamp hanging outside the saloon. Then he stood back and nodded, making Lincoln sigh with relief. He had blocked out his fears that he too might have succumbed, but this welcome news made him realize how tense the uncertainty had made him.

'Obliged,' he said.

'You're fine for now,' Weaver said, beckoning for Kyle to be brought forward, 'so you'll stay with the well people.'

'He was already,' Shelby said. 'I want him where I can see him.'

'But you wouldn't if he'd been ill,' Weaver said as he examined Kyle. 'Like this one is.'

'Are you sure?' Kyle murmured, his voice emerging as a strangulated gasp.

Weaver lowered his voice. 'I'm sorry, but you're showing the first signs.'

'What . . . what do I do?' Kyle said as Weaver moved backwards for a pace.

Within seconds a gap opened up around him. Kyle looked around, imploring someone to help him, but Weaver was the only one to meet his eye before he pointed.

'For a start,' Weaver said in a kindly tone, 'go to the wagon and join your comatose friend. Then you'll have to stay on the south side. I'm sorry, but you've paid a heavy price for delivering water to us.'

'I didn't know it was poisoned, but that's no excuse. I deserve this.' Kyle did as ordered and moved away.

Lincoln noted that this took him outside the circle of Shelby's men, although whether that was Weaver's plan he couldn't tell. Sadly, he now wondered if Weaver had no secret plan and that he was genuinely picking out the sick people.

Weaver then moved on to looking Gail over, making Peter tense and glare at his back as if he'd attack him despite the gun being held on him. But when he declared her healthy, Peter relaxed and stood tall as Weaver moved on to check him.

'This is the right policy,' Shelby said, nodding approvingly. 'Is there anything else you'd recommend I do?'

'Fetch me the barrel of water from the right-hand side of the wagon. I need to wash my hands frequently.'

Shelby balked at being given a direct order, but he picked two men to roll the barrel down, then place it on the boardwalk.

'Why that one?'

'I've already drunk from it and I don't want anyone but myself and Gail to use it. Isolating the water we use will stop the plague spreading if we get infected.'

Weaver finished checking Peter, then his forehead furrowed in a concerned frown.

Peter stared at him agog with shock, as did every-one else. Then those around him took quick steps backwards, giving Peter enough room to join Kyle at the wagon.

'I hid in a barrel of poisoned water,' Peter said. 'I suppose I shouldn't be surprised.'

'I'm going with him,' Gail said.

'Of course you can,' Weaver said, 'but I need you to help me care for everyone else too.' Weaver laid a hand on her shoulder, ensuring she couldn't go to her husband. 'I know it'll be hard, but if we all work together, he'll be fine.'

Peter reached the wagon and, standing beside Kyle, he joined his sick companion in lowering his head.

'But who else has it?' Shelby barked. 'The quicker you work this out, the better chance the rest of us have.'

A brief smile tugged at the corner of Weaver's mouth as Shelby accepted the urgency of the situation along with his authority and method.

Weaver started on the captors. He worked his way along them starting, deliberately to Lincoln's mind, with those standing furthest away from Shelby, thereby leaving him to last and making him sweat over the verdict.

Thankfully he declared each man to be fit, gradu-ally making the group relax but also making them glare at Peter, Kyle, and Nick, reinforcing that the division would work. Marvin and Shelby were the last ones for Weaver to check and, proving how nervous

124

he was getting, Shelby stepped forward to be checked first.

Everyone tensed, knowing that a bad verdict on Shelby's condition would test Weaver's policy, but Lincoln noted that Shelby's men were standing back, awaiting the decision with the cold eyes that only those who had been declared fit could offer.

As it turned out, Weaver patted his shoulder.

'You're fine,' he said. 'The measures you took worked and if we work together, they'll continue to do so.'

Shelby breathed deeply and rubbed at his face as he overcame his tension.

'Agreed,' Shelby said as Weaver moved on to check Marvin. 'We can prevail and that means nobody should be spared.'

'They shouldn't,' Weaver said, backing away. 'And that includes this one. He's ill.'

As the matter of his own health had been decided Shelby wasted no time in backing away and then ordering Marvin to go to the wagon. Marvin looked around at everyone, including Lincoln, desperately seeking support, but he received nothing but cold glares, raised guns, and a demand that he turn over his gun.

'This isn't over,' Marvin said as with reluctance he threw his gun to the ground. Then he moved over to join Peter and Kyle. When he approached the wagon he saw the prone Nick close to for the first time.

He jerked backwards for a pace, his surprise probably being noted and understood only by Lincoln.

125

Then, while smiling, he joined Peter.

Everyone then looked to Weaver to give them their next orders.

'Now the new Hope Wells regime starts,' Weaver said, moving over to join Gail. He looked at Peter across twenty yards of ground that might as well now be a mile. 'And it's one in which I give the orders.'

This time not even Shelby objected.

CHAPTER 15

Nick was being shaken.

He flexed his shoulders, knocking the hands away, and with some relief he noted that he could now move.

Light was filtering in around the edges of a door to his side proving that time had passed since he'd been carried away from the wagon. He must have slept through the night and despite the passage of time he didn't feel ill yet.

As he was now in the south side of the town, he probably wouldn't remain well for long. And there was the matter of the shaking.

He focused on the man looking down at him and with a gulp he recognized him.

'Marvin Sewell,' Nick croaked.

'So you're conscious enough to remember me,' Marvin said, grinning. 'I'm pleased. Now I can enjoy watching you die.'

Marvin moved his hands to Nick's neck and pressed in, closing his windpipe.

Nick was lying on the floor so he could brace his back, but weakened by Weaver's drug and sleep he could only twist ineffectually. Worse, Marvin had settled down on his chest and he was bearing down with grim determination.

Darkness clawed at Nick's vision. His lungs screamed for air. He grabbed Marvin's wrists but they were like iron and he couldn't move them.

The sinking sensation he'd had when Weaver had put a cloth over his mouth returned. But then, to his surprise, a cooling blast of air burst into his mouth. Not questioning his luck he gasped and floundered like a beached fish until he regained enough of his senses to see that he was now lying on his side.

He shuffled groggily to a sitting position to find that his saviour was Peter. He too had been placed in quarantine and he had pushed Marvin off him. Peter was now holding Marvin up against the wall with one hand on his chest and with the other bunched and held back ready to hit him if he fought back.

'Obliged,' Nick croaked.

'I owed you,' Peter said. 'I couldn't let you die too quickly.'

Nick acknowledged the bleak humour with a smile. Then tentatively he got to his feet. He found that he was stronger than he had feared he would be and, with a roll of the shoulders and a stretching of his legs, the numbness receded.

'How do you feel?' he asked.

'I feel fine.'

Peter gave Marvin a warning glare, then backed

away from him, but Marvin spoke up in a calm manner.

'I feel fine too.'

They had been placed together in a secure store-room. Sacks and crates surrounded them, leaving only a small living space.

To his knowledge Weaver hadn't identified anyone else as being sick overnight and that provided him with a faint hope that they wouldn't get ill, after all.

Perhaps in reality Weaver had incorrectly diag-nosed his companions for other reasons: Peter to separate him from Gail, and Marvin to get to the money he'd stolen.

That thought made him remember the other man Weaver had singled out. With a sinking feeling he looked around the room. Peter caught his eye and with a sombre expression he pointed to a pile of sacks in the corner; they had been fashioned into a sleeping area.

Kyle lay there; he was the only one of them who was sweaty and ill looking. Kyle had drunk the water a day before Nick had and now it was taking its toll.

'I got it first,' Kyle murmured when he sat beside him.

Nick struggled to reply, partly because he couldn't think of any comforting words for the young man, and partly because in his fevered eyes he saw the fate that awaited him.

'Rest,' he said, patting Kyle's clammy hand.

He turned to go, but Kyle murmured, encourag-ing him to return.

'If I die,' he said, 'make sure my story gets out.'

Nick doubted he'd live for long enough to keep the promise, but he nodded and the weak young man closed his eyes, appearing more contented than before. Nick stood and turned to face the concerned looking Peter and the surly Marvin.

'Where's the money you stole from the depot, Marvin?' Nick asked, deciding that dwelling on something other than death would provide welcome relief.

'I haven't got it.' Marvin nodded to the door. 'Shelby took it.'

Nick sneered. 'I'm pleased it didn't bring you good fortune. It certainly didn't help me. I lost my job.'

'I'm sorry, but I wasn't to know that Brad Ellison was dead.'

Although Nick had spent his journey here hating Marvin for double-crossing him in White Ridge, he saw the fear in his eyes and he felt a twinge of compassion for his predicament.

'Owing a man like Brad money must have been rough for you,' he said using a conciliatory tone.

'It was,' Marvin answered, conceding his mistake by raising his hands to tell Peter to let him pass. He sat by the wall where he considered Nick. 'I wish I'd found another way.'

'You should have come to me for the money.'

'You'd have refused.'

'I would, but you still should have come to me.'

Marvin smiled. 'I borrowed the money originally

to impress your sister and repay her past kindness. Without it she might not—'

'Stop making excuses,' Nick muttered advancing on him, 'or this time it'll be my hands at your throat.'

Marvin lowered his head, showing that he had been attempting to make his crime sound less serious than it had been, and it was left to Peter to step between them.

'If you two fight again, I'll leave you to it. As long as they take your bodies away I'll have a better chance of surviving.'

Nick winced, then looked from one man to the other, wondering whether to mention his theory that even if he and Kyle were doomed, Peter and Marvin might not be. But as their reactions were unpredictable, he settled for a simpler way of getting them on his side.

'You're right,' he said. 'We need to put aside our differences and fight back. And I reckon we can agree that the source of our troubles is Ward Dixon.'

Peter grunted that he agreed; when Marvin did the same Nick moved away from keeping the peace between them. The three men sat in a circle.

'If I'm to die,' Peter said, 'I want him to die first for endangering my wife.'

'And we have to do it quickly,' Marvin said, 'before we get too weak to take him on.'

Peter looked around the secure room. He shook his head at the magnitude of the endeavour.

'Agreed, but we're locked in, unarmed, and everyone in town is against us. Even if we can get out, how

131

can we launch an attack on a man who's holed up five miles out of town?'

When Marvin joined Peter in shaking his head, Nick raised a hand, gathering their attention.

'By using,' he said, 'those weaknesses to our advantage.'

'Every hour you hold me at gunpoint,' Lincoln said, peering at Shelby from the cell where he'd taken up residence, 'adds another year to your prison sentence.'

'Be quiet or I'll lock the door and throw away the key,' Shelby muttered.

This morning Weaver was carrying out a round of examinations with Gail. Shelby had given him access to his part of town and, there being people who hadn't been examined before to look over, he was taking longer than everyone's frayed nerves could cope with.

'And when Weaver returns, he'd better report that my prisoners are being cared for properly, otherwise you're looking at an even longer sentence.'

'You reckon I can let the Ellisons live?' Shelby spluttered, walking across the law office to stare at him, but Lincoln said nothing. 'They tried to kill this town, twice.'

'We don't know that for sure yet. The first time was probably an accident and as for the second occasion, let's hope Weaver has saved us in time.'

Shelby considered him. 'And if the situation is too bad for even Weaver to do anything?'

132

'Then the law will deal with them.' Lincoln watched Shelby narrow his eyes. 'On the other hand, if the plague's returned, none of us will live for long enough to care.'

Shelby accepted Lincoln's small concession with a nod, then left him.

The next hour passed tensely. Shelby paced the office and the four men with him spent less time watching their prisoner than they did looking out the window for Weaver.

At noon Lincoln asked for coffee. When he got a snapped response to fetch it himself, he did so, then settled down in a spare chair outside the cell to drink it.

Shelby accepted his new position without comment; he and his men were armed and Lincoln wasn't.

Another hour passed before Shelby at last gave in to his nerves and sent a man off to find out what was happening. The messenger returned quickly with news.

'Marvin, Nick and Peter have escaped,' he said. 'Weaver is searching for them.'

'He shouldn't be doing that,' Shelby said. 'That's my responsibility. Get him back here to report on the job he should be doing while you round up ten men to find them.'

'And when they do?'

'Shoot them and bury the bodies quickly. They can't be allowed to spread their filth.'

The man hurried out, leaving Shelby to glance

with raised eyebrows at Lincoln, requesting his opinion.

'They'll be long gone,' Lincoln said. 'Leave it to Ward to find them.'

In truth Lincoln reckoned that only Marvin would have run; the others would be working to free him. Shelby returned a cryptic smile that suggested he'd discerned his true feelings, but before Lincoln could trade words with him the man returned with Weaver and Gail in tow.

'And?' Shelby barked the moment Weaver came through the door.

'The situation's promising,' Weaver said, sitting on the edge of a desk. 'The four men to catch it last night are the only new ones suffering. The one man not to run, Kyle, is dying, so we have to find the other three quickly.'

'I will, now that you've informed me of the situation.' Shelby pointed at him. 'Do not withhold information from me again.'

'And do not question my actions again or you'll be the next to fall ill.'

Shelby didn't reply immediately, seemingly lost for words. He narrowed his eyes, but then he dismissed the thought he appeared to have had with a shake of the head.

'Have a coffee,' he said, pointing to the stove. 'Then we'll discuss this like rational men.'

Weaver cast a disdainful look at the stove and the barrel of water that had been brought in. He shook his head, then turned back to Shelby.

'I prefer to stick to water I've seen poured out.'

Shelby nodded. 'I reckon we'll all find it hard to trust water again.'

Shelby went to the stove and filled a mug. He offered Lincoln a refill; he refused it, so he turned to Gail. She shook her head, then removed the barrel lid and looked around for a mug.

'Perhaps, but you need to trust me just as I need to trust you.' Weaver had been looking at Lincoln while Shelby was at the stove and he waited until Shelby came back into his eyeline before continuing. 'So what are your orders?'

'Get some rest. I reckon today and tomorrow will be fraught.'

Weaver sighed. 'It'll be a tiring time for me and Gail.'

Weaver moved off the desk. He looked for Gail, finding her looking out of the window while nursing her mug of water. Weaver did a double-take. Then, with a pained screech, he dashed across the room.

Gail turned to find Weaver swiping a wild blow at her that dashed the mug from her hands and sent the water splashing against the wall.

'Why. . . ?' she murmured, aghast.

Weaver grabbed her arms.

'Did you drink the water?' he demanded. When she stared at him in shock he shook her then clutched her to his chest before shaking her again. 'Did you? Did you?'

'I didn't, but. . . .'

Weaver breathed a sigh of relief, then patted her

shoulder and released her. He turned to find that everyone was staring at him.

'What are you panicking about?' Shelby asked. 'She only drank the water you brought back from the creek.'

'She did,' Weaver said, his voice cracking. He coughed to clear his throat. 'I've been on edge recently and, like you said, we'll all find it hard to trust water again.'

Shelby forced a laugh, then bade Weaver to join him.

Weaver left the still bemused Gail and walked across the office, meeting everyone's eye in turn with shamefaced looks. He received supportive nods from everyone, but when he looked at Lincoln, the lawman rose to his feet.

Lincoln emptied his own mug of coffee on to the floor, then went to the water barrel. He walked slowly, ensuring that everyone was watching him, then dipped the mug inside.

'It will be hard,' he said, then held out the mug to Weaver. 'So drink this down now and get over your fears.'

CHAPTER 16

'No further,' one rider said. 'Turn back while you still can.'

Peter and Marvin separated, as they'd agreed, and put on pleasant smiles while spreading their arms.

'We're not trouble,' Peter said. 'We just want to talk to you about the water.'

'No more water until you pay.'

The second of the two riders laughed.

'And,' he said, 'the cost has gone up again.'

Peter stepped forward with an unconcerned expression on his face; this made both riders edge forward, moving to within thirty yards of him. Thankfully this moved them past the spot where Nick was hiding in the shadow of a mound, so he stood quietly then walked sideways to stand behind them.

Peter kept them talking, spinning a tale about how they needed the barrels delivered at sunup rather than later in the day. The riders weren't co-operative, but they did listen, and that was all Nick needed.

He edged towards the nearest rider while Marvin

played his part by moving in the opposite direction, to force the men to turn and watch him.

'No further,' one rider said.

'I wasn't doing nothing,' Marvin said.

'Then get back and join. . . .' The rider pointed at Peter, but then he leaned forward to consider him. 'You're the man who tried to get in earlier. How did you get to Hope Wells?'

Nick reckoned Peter's and Marvin's distracting tactic had achieved everything it could do. He hurried on.

He covered ten paces before the rider saw him and jerked to the side, but he moved too slowly and he couldn't avoid Nick slapping both hands on a leg. Fuelled on by desperation Nick dragged him from the saddle.

He and the rider fell entangled with the rider landing heavily. The man used up valuable moments shaking Nick off him, and by the time he'd freed himself he was too late. Nick had the man's six-shooter in hand and he was backing away to keep him and the seated rider in view.

'You'll regret this,' the man on the ground said, shaking himself as if that could remove the taint of having been touched.

'And you're not leaving,' the rider said, training his gun on Nick.

'They were telling the truth,' Nick said. 'We really do want to talk about the water.'

Nick doubted he'd be able to fight off both men; the gun he'd secured gave him no advantage other

than the trust it could buy him. With an unconcerned expression he dropped it, making the two
men nod approvingly.

'Go on,' the rider said, lowering his own gun.

'Doctor Weaver's planning to double-cross Ward.
He wants a bigger cut of the money for himself.'

'He didn't want money,' the man on the ground
said.

'He does now,' Nick said with as much assurance
as he could muster after his mistake. 'If he doesn't
get what he wants, he'll lead the townsfolk in a break-
out. Unless Ward acts now this disease will get out.'

'We don't care about that.' The man considered
for a moment, then looked at the rider. They silently
discussed the matter with raised eyebrows and ges-
tures until he turned back. 'But rest assured, Ward
will deal with Weaver.'

'I don't need a drink,' Weaver said, eyeing the brimming mug of water with undisguised loathing. 'I had
my fill outside.'

Lincoln smiled. 'From the water barrel that only
you and Gail use?'

Weaver avoided Lincoln's eye. 'I've explained why
I did that. Cleanliness is important and I don't want
to spread the disease.'

Several people nodded, but Shelby leaned forward
to consider him showing that he had also detected
Weaver's evasiveness.

'I agree,' Lincoln said, speaking loudly to address
everyone in the room. 'We shouldn't drink the water

you and Gail use, just like we didn't with the first water shipment. But I don't see why you shouldn't use our water.'

Weaver grunted something under his breath and waved a dismissive hand at him. He turned away and with what Lincoln viewed as an exaggerated slouch to encourage sympathy for his hard work and devotion he moved over to a chair and slumped down on to it.

Several men glanced at each other and shrugged, but when Lincoln turned to Shelby he was already looking at him and nodding.

'Weaver,' he said, his tone low and commanding, 'put Lincoln's suspicious mind at ease and drink the water.'

Weaver gave a very evident gulp. 'Why?'

'To show us that you know it's safe.'

'It is. Don't doubt me. One word from me and you'll join the dying.'

Weaver's right eye twitched, perhaps showing that he knew he'd erred with this threat. One of Shelby's men stood, as did another man, their brows furrowing as the worrying thought that had hit Lincoln took hold.

'So,' Shelby said, his voice growing in confidence as he noticed the change in atmosphere, 'is that what happened to Peter, Marvin, Kyle and Nick? Did they cross you, and so you had them removed?'

Weaver moved over to the barrel and slapped it.

'You're twisting my words. I meant you shouldn't cross the only man who can save you.'

Shelby stood up and made his way across the room towards him.

'Fine words from a doctor, a man who should save everyone whether they've crossed him or not.'

Weaver looked around for support. He didn't get it, and when he faced the window Gail was walking towards him too.

'Don't worry,' she said. 'I trust you. I know the strain you've been under and the terrible things you've had to deal with. These men have no right to turn on you.'

Weaver breathed a sigh of relief and placed a hand on her shoulder.

'Thank you,' he said, lowering his head.

Gail met everyone's eyes and defied them to continue making him feel uncomfortable. Nobody responded, so she fetched the mug that Weaver had dashed from her hands earlier and went to the barrel.

'So,' she said, 'I'll show how much I trust you by drinking.'

Weaver stared at her open-mouthed, shaking his head.

'No,' he whispered, his voice barely audible, but it was loud enough to make Shelby shake a fist in triumph and for Lincoln to move in.

Weaver moved to wrest the mug from her, but she jerked away. He reached out to her, but Lincoln had already stepped up to him and he grabbed his collar, then yanked him backwards.

With surprising strength Weaver tore himself away

from Lincoln's grip. He looked at Gail, but she had turned away, her shoulders hunched as she sobbed. As everyone else closed in he ran for the door. He bundled two men aside to reach it, then hurried out on to the boardwalk.

'Nobody drink the water!' Lincoln said, standing before the barrel. 'It's poisoned. Weaver's the one who's been trying to destroy the town, not the Ellison brothers.'

'Why?' Shelby murmured.

Lincoln moved into Gail's eyeline and she cast him a sorrowful look.

'Because of me,' she said. 'He once asked me to leave Peter, but I refused. Then this crisis hit and he needed me. But it'd end soon and I'd go back to Rocky Bar. I guess he never wanted it to end.'

'It's not your fault.' Lincoln cast her a consoling smile, then turned to Shelby. 'But it's your last chance to decide who the enemy is.'

Shelby took a deep breath. 'It's anyone who breaks the law. The Ellisons aren't to blame for this, but plenty of old scores were settled last night. You can have what's left of them.'

'In that case it's time this town started pulling together.'

Shelby gulped. 'But we all drank Weaver's poisoned water. We'll die.'

'We don't know that for sure yet. From what I've seen the town was getting better despite what Weaver was doing. Perhaps the disease has run its course.' Lincoln raised his voice as the idea took hold and he started to believe it himself. 'Perhaps Brad Ellison's body has done all the harm it'll ever do and we won't get sick.'

This statement encouraged several supportive comments and with renewed purpose Shelby went to the armoury. He removed Lincoln's six-shooter and handed it to him.

'What's your orders?' he asked.

'We get Weaver. Then we get water from the creek. Then we get better.'

'And the cordon?'

'It dies today, and so will Ward Dixon if he gets in my way.'

Lincoln strode on to the door where he stopped to ensure that everyone was following him. Then he paced out on to the boardwalk to find that an unexpected development had taken place.

A line of riders was blocking the end of the road. Weaver had stopped in front of them and was gesticulating wildly. For their part the riders were glaring down at him with aggrieved menace.

'If I'm guessing this aright,' Shelby said from behind Lincoln, 'one part of our mission has just got easier.'

Lincoln nodded. 'Yeah. It seems that Ward Dixon has saved us a journey.'

CHAPTER 17

'Everything's changed for Weaver,' Peter said, watching the doctor standing before Ward and the rest of his men.

'Yeah,' Marvin said. 'He's struggling to explain himself.'

Nick watched the conversation for another minute. From the safety of the stables on the edge of town he was too far away to hear what was being said, but he had to agree with his colleagues.

It wasn't just that the doctor had been forced to confront Ward; he was agitated and he wasn't acting in his usual calm manner.

Peter drew Nick forward to look down the road, where he saw the likely reason why.

Marshal Lincoln Hawk had brought everyone out on to the road. Unlike the impression Nick had got when he'd been drugged that everyone was at each other's throats, now everyone appeared to have a common sense of purpose.

Lincoln was pointing to spots around town, ordering the group to split up. Keeping in the shadows these men moved away, following his instructions without question. But they weren't stealthy enough to avoid Ward's gaze.

He broke off from his discussion with Weaver to survey the scene. Then with an overhead gesture he bade his men to retreat.

'It's a trap,' he shouted. 'Weaver's already organized them.'

'I haven't,' Weaver shouted. 'We can still work together to—'

Without warning Ward fired at the doctor, making him drop to his knees. His hands rose to clutch his stomach.

Then, with a muttered growl of anguish, Weaver fought his way to his feet. He looked back down the road, his gaze seeking out the law office, but his action instigated a sustained volley of gunshots from Ward's men that tore into his back and made him writhe, then collapse.

Peter's grunt of approval suggested to Nick that Weaver had been looking for a last sighting of Gail rather than planning to signal to Lincoln, but that didn't matter to Ward; he fired down at him until he stilled. Then he hollered at his men and they turned to head out of town.

They'd yet to move on when gunfire blasted out from beyond the edge of town. One rider fell from his horse while another cried out in pain. The other men struggled to control their mounts as they searched for the source of the shooting.

Faced with an unknown number of gunmen hiding in the dark, Ward backed his horse away, then beckoned for everyone to follow him to the nearest cover of the stables.

'Time to move on,' Nick said.

He, along with Peter and Marvin, was standing by the main door. He retreated into the shadows, then looked for a way out. Nick couldn't see one, so he took one side of the stables while Peter took the other. Nick hurried down his side. He had proved there wasn't a way out when Peter got his attention with an urgent grunt.

More light streamed into the stables as Peter opened a side door and slipped through it. Nick and Marvin hurried after him. They had to run across the open area and when Nick looked to the road the riders were closing on the main door while others dismounted and spread out.

At the door he moved to follow Peter out, but then he slid to a halt when a different man appeared in the doorway. Each looked at the other with surprise.

Nick was the first to get over his shock and he bundled the man away, then turned to go in the same direction as Peter had gone. But a second man was standing there, watching the fleeing Peter.

This man reacted quickly and he moved to bar Nick's way. As the other man gathered his wits about him they combined forces to push Nick back into the stables.

Nick looked to Marvin for help, but he had backed

away from the door. Then he hurried into the centre of the stables to face Ward as he rode in through the door.

'I'm Marvin Sewell,' he called. 'I have money and I'm with you.'

'That's one of the men who told us to come here to stop Weaver,' a rider said, turning his horse to face the door.

'I did, but it was the others who wanted to trap you. I didn't.'

Ward said nothing as he dismounted, but Nick couldn't keep quiet.

'That was your last chance,' he muttered, 'you good-for-nothing double-crosser.'

He shook off a hand that landed on his shoulder. Then with determined paces he walked up to Marvin, who heard him coming and turned with an apologetic expression on his face. But that only annoyed Nick even more. He broke into a run, then aimed a scything punch at Marvin's face.

Marvin swayed away from the fist, but it still caught him a glancing blow to the cheek that rocked him sideways. He stood bent double then shook himself and leapt at Nick.

The two men tussled, now oblivious to Ward's arrival and the developing situation outside.

Nick reckoned he'd given Marvin all the chances he ever would; now he'd make him pay. Within moments the two men were on the ground. They rolled back and forth across the hard-packed dirt, delivering kicks and short-armed punches.

Nick was aware of Ward's men spreading out to surround them, but they didn't try to stop their fight. Instead, Ward shouted orders and his men scurried to take up positions by the main door.

Clearly the siege was coming to a head, and thinking about the impending battle made some of Nick's anger drain away.

He fought his way clear of Marvin's clutches and got to his feet while backing away, but Marvin kicked off from the ground, then ran into him. His momentum drove Nick backwards for several paces.

Nick tried to dig in his heels but he failed and he went tumbling, his motion rolling him out through the main door and into the road.

'Give me a gun,' Marvin shouted, 'and I'll take them all on for you.'

On the ground Nick shook himself and looked up to see Marvin standing in the doorway with his hands spread, imploring Ward to help him.

'Don't trust him,' Nick shouted. 'He'll turn on you like he turned on me.'

Ward considered Nick, then gestured for someone to throw Marvin a gun. A few seconds later a six-shooter was handed out from the doorway, but perhaps deliberately the thrower launched the weapon past Marvin's outstretched hands. It skidded to a halt ten feet beyond him and slightly further away from Nick's clutches.

As Marvin set off for it Nick wasted no time in rolling to his feet. Marvin was ahead of him, but Nick kept going and the moment Marvin reached the weapon and bent to scoop it up Nick leapt at him. He wrapped his arms around his hips from behind and pushed him on.

He couldn't stop Marvin picking up the weapon, but since his opponent had his back to him he couldn't be shot. The two men shuffled round on the spot, kicking up dust as Marvin tried to wrest himself free of Nick's grasp.

Nick knew that the moment he succeeded he was doomed.

Their scuffling circular passage let him see that the townsfolk had surrounded the stables, trapping Ward. With his confidence growing he slapped a hand on Marvin's gun arm, held it tightly, then released his other arm. His action let Marvin spin round, but at the same time Nick thrust Marvin's hand up high.

A gunshot flew skyward. Then as Marvin dragged the gun down a second shot ripped into the stable roof. The two men stared at each other.

Marvin's eyes were wide and troubled as he fought to gain the upper hand, but Nick could return only a look of disgust. Something in his eyes must have affected his opponent as he tensed, giving Nick a chance to thrust the arm up again.

'You've never given me a proper chance,' Marvin snapped. 'You never wanted me working for you.'

'Who could blame me? You caused my sister nothing but problems and you'd been in jail.'

'You should have believed me when I said I never wanted to go back there.'

'Except that's the only place you're going. You can't win. Either you'll get sent there for stealing from the depot or you'll get sent there for helping Ward.'

'I will not go back!'

'Then do the right thing for once and you might not.'

Marvin glared at him, but after straining and making no headway the plea appeared to get through to him. He softened his expression and lowered his voice.

'Let me have the gun. Trust me this one last time.'

A glazed look overcame Marvin's eyes as he gathered a renewed burst of strength. Nick tried to stop the gun from lowering, but he couldn't and it closed on him. He judged it'd be aimed at his head within seconds, but then the gun stopped and Marvin looked at him, his earnest gaze appearing to say he could move it if he chose to, but that he wouldn't.

Despite all Marvin's failings, Nick decided to trust him, although he didn't feel he had a choice. He gave a slight nod then released his grip. The gun jerked downwards as did Marvin.

Nick backed away as with a great roar, Marvin swung round to the stables. Several men were in sight and he swung the gun up and peppered gunfire at them. One man, then a second slumped to the ground before others emerged to confront him.

Gunfire blasted and, with no way to help him, Nick dived aside then rolled. When he came to a halt it was to see Marvin toppling over. But his suicidal bravery at the last had spurred the townsfolk on.

From all directions men were hurrying closer. The battle for the town had begun.

'There's only one other way out of the stables,' Peter said, 'and you've got that covered.'

Lincoln nodded, then directed Peter to join him in taking up a position side-on to the main stable door. They hunkered down behind a group of barrels, where Lincoln saw that Nick had scurried into safety, although Marvin lay prone and still.

'You're surrounded, Ward,' he shouted, 'and our cordon is solid. If you move five yards away from the stables, you're dead men.'

His warning made the townsfolk add their own taunts as they enjoyed seeing the tables turned on Ward.

'Quit gloating,' Ward shouted from the stables. 'I may be trapped here, but none of you can leave either. When the Rocky Bar folk hear about this they'll start a new cordon. You'll all still die.'

'But we'll see you die first.'

'You won't. You men don't know how to break through a cordon.'

Lincoln couldn't think of a retort, but he didn't need to. Ward had only traded insults to provide a distraction. Riders came surging out of the stables. They speeded rapidly to a gallop and this time they took a route through town.

Their sudden arrival took the townsfolk by sur-

151

prise and most of the riders had emerged before they got their wits about them and started shooting. But that was the moment when Ward's riders laid down a sustained volley of rapid gunfire directed at both sides of the main drag.

Despite their cover the gunfire was fierce enough to force the townsfolk to dive to safety. Ward himself picked out Lincoln's and Peter's position and blasted lead at them, holing the barrels and forcing them to stay down.

By the time Lincoln risked looking up the riders had burst through the ring of men surrounding the stables and a clear passage to the edge of town was ahead.

Lincoln loosed off a couple of shots at the backs of the fleeing riders. One shot found a home and sent a rider falling sideways from his saddle, but the rest quickly moved out of range. Lincoln jumped to his feet and gave chase, even though the effort felt futile.

Then he skidded to a halt with a grim smile on his lips.

Shelby had returned to his side of town and from the safety of the crossroads that he'd guarded so resolutely for the last week he gave the order to open fire. The men who had been on tenterhooks for all that time, waiting for the order to act, needed no second command.

With lethal ferocity they hammered lead at the riders.

Man after man went down. With the townsfolk in

good positions in the buildings and around the cross-roads, none of the returned gunfire lessened the fierceness of the deadly rain of lead. In a matter of seconds five riders were lying sprawled and holed on the ground, forcing Ward to accept that he wouldn't get past.

He waved overhead ordering everyone to turn back.

'Try the other way!' he shouted.

By the time he'd turned to make his desperate escape attempt Lincoln had paced out into the centre of the road, his six-shooter raised and aimed at him.

Ward was too far away for Lincoln to see his expression, but he reckoned Ward was smiling as he urged his horse on, aiming directly for him. Others loosed off speculative shots at the approaching riders, but Lincoln stayed his fire, letting Ward gallop closer, then loom over him.

Ward appeared as if he was only interested in running him down. But when he was within seconds of reaching him he jerked his gun up with his free hand and tore the reins to the side with the other hand.

Lincoln fired, aiming at the centre of Ward's body. Despite his target's speed the shot hit home before Ward could fire, catching his shoulder.

Lincoln followed him with his gun as Ward passed by, his arms waving as he struggled to stay upright in the saddle. Lincoln didn't shoot and he saw that he had been right to hold his fire when Ward slid from the saddle to tumble to the ground in a cloud of dust.

Lincoln watched him as from the corner of his eye he noted that the other riders were finding their route to the plains blocked. Shelby had sent a dozen men out of town and now that they were all in position they needed no encouragement to make their presence known. Sustained gunfire rattled out.

One rider tried to gallop into the darkness, but multiple shots from unseen gunmen dispatched him, while another was holed and sent tumbling from the saddle by a single shot from a hotel window opposite the stables. That sight proved to be too much for the other two riders. They both thrust up arms in surrender while drawing their mounts to a halt.

Lincoln paced down the road to stand over the wounded Ward, who scrambled for his dropped six-shooter with his left hand. But while his hand was still clawing across the ground, Lincoln kicked the gun away. He waited for Ward to look up before he spoke.

'It seems,' Lincoln said with a smile, 'that you don't know how to break through a cordon either.'

Ward conceded his point with a shrug that made him wince.

'I made money, but Weaver made everyone ill,' Ward said with a resigned smile, his eyes now pleading as he accepted his fate. 'I killed him for you. That has to count for something.'

Lincoln aimed down at him and firmed his gun hand, making Ward cringe and try to move away.

'Yeah, it means you're condemned to suffer the worst punishment of all.' Lincoln lowered the gun. 'You'll stay here and die with the rest of us.'

CHAPTER 18

Ward stood before the barrel, his two surviving men flanking him. He stared straight ahead, clearly trying to avoid giving anyone the satisfaction of seeing him squirm.

Not that anyone wanted this to be the way the siege at Hope Wells ended. Lincoln detected no triumphant feelings now that the townsfolk had at last freed themselves.

The deaths here had demoralized everyone too much for that.

Lincoln caught Shelby's eye and beckoned for him to act. So Shelby dunked a mug in the barrel, then held it out.

With as much dignity as he could muster Ward took the mug and looked down at the water. A tremor made the brimming water spill on to the ground.

'Just the one mug?' he asked.

'Just the one,' Shelby said. 'Then Lincoln will throw you in a cell and you can spend your last hours

156

knowing what it's like to die in pain after you've killed the only man who could have saved you.'

'And if I don't drink?'

'You will.'

Ward met Shelby's firm gaze. Then he looked at Nick, who saluted him with a casual wave. With arrogant defiance Ward downed the water in one gulp, only his subsequent involuntary shiver showing he wasn't as composed as he was trying to appear.

He returned the mug to Shelby, who moved on to making the other two survivors from Ward's group drink. They weren't as stoical as Ward had been and they needed to be held firmly while Shelby poured the water down their throats.

When this operation had been completed and the three prisoners stood bowed and defeated Nick joined Lincoln. Both men frowned acknowledging their distaste at completing the process of turning the tables on Ward. But the townsfolk, who had suffered for longer than they had, mustered a few jeers, proving that this had been the right way to release the tension that had built up.

Then, to Lincoln's gestured instructions, Shelby dragged the prisoners off to the law office to put them in the cell beside the Ellison brothers.

Lincoln consoled himself with the thought that Shelby's action was another sign of the authority of the law returning to Hope Wells. Pleasingly, that process had taken a giant leap forward a few minutes ago with the revelations made by the Ellison brothers. Their freely provided statement had saved

Ward's life, even if he didn't know it yet.

It seemed that when everyone had got sick, the brothers had dragged Brad's body out of the well and buried him, hoping they'd get away with his murder. They'd created the muddiness around the wells when they'd tried to flush them out so that they could again provide a clean water supply.

Lincoln had no way of knowing for sure, but it was likely that their actions had ultimately lessened the effects of the poisoned water. It was also likely that if it hadn't been for Weaver's actions, the town would have recovered more quickly.

'You reckon this is over?' Lincoln said.

Nick nodded. 'I feel fine and I drank a lot of water. So I hope the disease has run its course.'

Lincoln smiled. 'And until Ward finds that out, it should make him appreciate how much he made the people here suffer.'

'It will.' Nick looked east, his distant gaze showing that he was relishing leaving later when it was safe to do so. 'What are you planning to do now?'

'I'll stay to keep the peace until a proper lawman can be appointed. And you?'

'Kyle died,' Nick said in a sombre tone, 'but he died to get Hope Wells's story told and that shouldn't be forgotten. As soon as I can leave I'll ensure that his account of how this town nearly died appears in the *North Town Times*.'

Lincoln slapped him on the back, then moved away. Already people were milling around, clearing away the bodies, and Peter and Gail were talking contentedly as Hope Wells showed more life than it had done since he arrived.

'Except there's another story yet to be told,' Lincoln said approvingly, 'of how this town was reborn.'

With that thought cheering him, Lincoln headed to the law office to give the good news to his prisoners.